FAILING MEN SAVING WOMEN

IAN MEACHEAM

APS BOOKS
Yorkshire

APS Books,
The Stables Field Lane,
Aberford,
West Yorkshire,
LS25 3AE

APS Books is a subsidiary of the APS Publications imprint

www.andrewsparke.com

First published worldwide by APS Books in 2023

A catalogue record for this book is available from the British Library

To Ann
always and forever

Other books by Ian Meacheam

An Inspector Called
Time And The Consequences
Broad Lines Narrow Margins
Reading Rites Writing Wrong
Shining Light Dark Matter
Stone People Glass Houses
Seven Stages *(with Mark Peckett)*

CONTENTS

I
LIVING THE LIVES

THE DOOR

Part One

Maureen lifted the tray from her lap and placed it next to her on the settee. She'd enjoyed the simple meal that she'd produced. Half a tin of baked beans on one piece of toast and a scrambled egg on the other. Also on the tray was a peach yoghurt and a mug of tea. She had consumed the lot while she watched the evening national and regional news on the television. She thought that she might have a small glass of wine later or a bar of chocolate or even both - once she'd enjoyed Emmerdale and Eastenders. She had the evenings to herself these days. She could relax. 'Chill Time' - as her children would say.

For the first time in…forever…Maureen could properly chill, now that the funeral was out of the way and her son and daughter had returned to their own busy lives with their own families. Although she loved Mark and Grace, she was quite relieved when they both announced to their mother that they had to return to work. They both felt awful for leaving their mother on her own in the family house only a week after the funeral, but Maureen insisted that she would be fine.

Since they left, Mark and Grace had face-timed their mom religiously once or twice a week to see how she was coping. Maureen's children clearly worried about her state of mind. How would she cope on her own after sharing the house with their dad for thirty years, and up until eight years ago with her children as well, before they flew the nest.

The truth was, Maureen was enjoying her newly found freedom. Yes, the house seemed quiet and empty. But actually, she liked it like that. She liked the fact that she was in control. She could make her own decisions. No-one would disagree or argue with her.

Maureen kept this all to herself. It would sound uncaring and selfish to her friends and family. It wasn't as if she didn't love her children, or Derek for that matter. She loved her children and her grandchildren. But both Grace and then Mark had found their own chosen ones to love and have a family with. And those newly-formed nests became more important than the old nest that they had flown from.

It was only a year or so after Maureen and Derek adjusted to a relatively quiet life that Derek started to become ill. It was a slow process and a slow decline. They kept it from their kids for a year or two. They both lived a distance away from their mother and father and didn't need the worry. It was only when Derek's hair started falling out and the treatment wasn't showing any positive

signs of improvement, that they were told. Weekend visits were made as often as the kids and grandkids could manage.

Maureen reduced her hours in her job so that she could look after Derek. She had loved her responsibility at work but now she was relegated to an office administrator, three hours a day. She found the adjustment at work challenging but also the change of lifestyle at home. She became a part-time nurse, administering medication to her husband, part-time carer, responding to his hygienic needs and part-time chef, catering for his dietary needs. Maureen wasn't the most patient of nurses, carers or chefs, but Derek was not the easiest patient to look after. He was demanding, awkward and downright unpleasant at times. Maureen, at times, could sympathise and understand why this big, strong man felt so frustrated. He had lost weight, considerable mobility, and his joie de vivre.

But these were the cards that Maureen had been dealt and she loved her husband in sickness and in health, most of the time. So, she tried to keep calm and carry on. Occasionally, when Derek was feeling slightly better, Maureen could leave Derek and spend a few hours at the weekend, shopping or visiting some local friends for a cup of tea and a cake. She needed to escape from time to time, if only to better cope with her time inside the house.

That freedom stopped just over eighteen months ago. Derek's decline accelerated and the visiting doctors started to talk in terms of months rather than years. Maureen reduced her hours at work even further and her job description as nurse, carer and chef increased. Maureen kept her children informed and occasionally Derek managed a phone call to them and the grandchildren. Initially there were weekly visits from professionals to assist Maureen, which gradually increased to daily visits within four months. The prognosis was now down to weeks rather than months. Stop-overs from Grace and Mark became regular events when they could free up the time to visit. The house was busy with well-meaning and caring people.

But it so happened that on the day of Derek's passing, Maureen was on her own with him in the house. She had given up work on compassionate grounds and was preparing her husband the medicinal cocktail for him to drink in his sippy cup. On returning to his bedroom, she could sense that Derek would no longer be needing the medicine. Maureen had turned her back on him for five minutes and Derek had decided that this was the time to leave her.

Over the next couple of weeks, the house was very busy, initially with ambulance crew, doctors, and then with family, friends, neighbours, ex-work colleagues, funeral directors and the local vicar who would be overseeing the funeral. All well-meaning and supportive do-gooders and well-wishers. Grace co-ordinated the funeral, Mark took charge of all things financial, and Maureen was left to answer the door, put flowers in vases and make cups of tea for visitors.

The funeral was as good as a funeral can ever be and the gathering afterwards at Derek's old golf club was well-organised and respectful. Maureen had received so many heart-felt good wishes, kisses and hugs by the end of the day that she was emotionally drained. She wanted to sleep for a week but her children, their partners and their children were occupying the two spare bedrooms and the dining room. It was a huge relief when the day came when they all considered that the time was right to leave her on her own. They were, after all, only a phone call away.

That was five months ago. Maureen had the house back to herself. Her house. Of course, there were reminders of Derek all over the place. The house felt empty without him but strangely she did not want too many reminders on show. So, she systematically changed the décor to make it her place. Derek's remaining 'stuff' went to charity shops or into the loft.

The house gradually changed and so did Maureen's old routines which had been determined over the last 30 years. Now, there was a blank sheet to form her new action plan:

Cook only things that she liked to eat.
Eat at the times she wanted to eat.
Leave the washing up until she fancied doing it.
Have a glass of wine in the evening, if she felt like it.
Watch TV programmes that she wanted to watch without criticisms.
Cancel SKY Sports.
Have a thick duvet on the bed all year round.
Have a long leisurely bath occasionally.
Wear pyjamas during the evening.

Phone friends at any time.

Go for a walk when it suited.

Enjoy clothes shopping without guilt or moaning in the background.

Maureen began to enjoy this freedom to live her new life, but she found it difficult to admit it, even to her children. It wasn't as if Derek was a monster. He could be kind and supportive at times. He could be thoughtful and generous at other times. But those times were less frequent as the years went by.

She was not heartless though. She still had feelings for Derek and some treasured memories. There had been times over those last five months when Maureen inexplicably felt sad and cried while she was watching TV or cooking a meal. There were also occasions, particularly in the quiet of evenings, when she would talk to her dead husband.

The days were OK. She visited friends or they visited her, she generally phoned friends during the day or went to the shops. The nights were lonely though. Most of her friends were still fortunate to be with their partners and stayed in their own homes in the evenings. If invited out in the evening by a couple, Maureen felt a little uncomfortable about being the odd-one-out in their company. Mostly, soap operas and the news were her night-time companions. They didn't necessarily make her happy, because of the depressing content of the programmes, but it filled her living room with the sound of living people.

One day, when visiting a friend, Maureen unexpectedly shed a tear and explained how quiet the house was and how lonely she felt in the evenings. Her practical friend hugged her while providing Maureen with a range of ideas to make her feel less lonely. These included – joining a gym, the University of the Third Age, or a dating site.

In the days that followed, Maureen discovered that most of the classes for the gym or U3A were during the day which did not solve her problem. When Grace visited her mother next, Maureen introduced the notion of joining a dating site specifically for older people looking for companionship. Grace, rather surprisingly, was not just in favour of it but helped her mother fill in the application form and download a couple of photographs on to Meet My Match.com.

In the next month or two and after various awkward and awful moments online or on the phone, Maureen had agreed to meet a man, a local divorced man, who had sounded pleasant enough. They had made it clear to one another that this was a 'friendship only' arrangement. They had discussed on the phone that he would pick her up from her house at 8.00 pm and would not be invited into her house before or after the meal at a local restaurant.

On the day before the 'date', Grace had insisted that her mother should supply her with all the known details concerning the man and the restaurant arrangements.

On the day of the 'date', Maureen had a long bath, chose a 'going out' dress that had been neglected in her wardrobe for at least five years and spent a little time on her hair and make-up. When she looked at herself in the mirror, Maureen did not recognise herself but smiled at the stranger.

At 7.59 pm, Maureen received a text.

I'm outside the front door. I hope you open it when I ring the bell.

Part Tw

Colin stood at the front door. It was cold tonight. But he was shivering with nervous excitement mixed in with terror as he waited for the door to open. He hoped the door would open. If the door remained shut, it wouldn't be the first time that Meet My Match would have disappointed him. Since he divorced his wife, now ex-wife, five years ago, he had not had any luck with this dating site. Two 'no-shows' at restaurants, one date that lasted less than two hours, and one woman who wanted a 'friend' as well as continuing to be married.

Colin thought that he was old enough and wise enough to identify time-wasters, but he was slowly coming to the conclusion that he would never meet a woman that he could trust and love. He was hoping beyond hope that Maureen would be the one that he could trust and share a platonic friendship with, at least.

Colin stood there asking himself how it had come to this.

He was 57 years old. He had a grown-up daughter and two grandchildren. He was a manager at a car showroom. A confident and sociable type. And yet at this very moment he felt like an awkward teenager about to ask his secret sweetheart in class if she would go the movies with him. His mind flashed back to that very scenario over forty years ago when the girl in question answered the doorbell and politely smiled and said, 'No thank you,' before closing the door on his hopes and dreams.

His relationships with girls, then young women and then women in their twenties were not that successful or long-lasting until he was nearing his thirties.

By then he was a car salesman. Earning a reasonable wage and commission. He still lived with his parents, which was difficult at times, but it helped him save for a mortgage on his own house to go with the rather nice car he drove. His manager at the showroom gave him a very good deal as Colin was his 'number one' salesman.

One day, in walked a woman in her mid-twenties looking to buy her first car since passing her test. She needed a simple run-around as she had just qualified as a nurse and didn't want to rely on public transport taking her to and from the hospital with the shifts she would be doing.

Normally, Colin would give a punter the patter and try to get them to buy something well above their means, but when he started to engage with Jess, he treated her differently. It wasn't just because of her good looks and pleasing personality, but because she seemed a little naïve. This would normally be an open goal for Colin, but not with Jess. He pointed out the second-hand cars that were in her price range and suitable, and those that she should avoid. Jess took two cars on a test drive with Colin and with his advice about the better deal, she filled in the monthly payment paperwork on a three-year-old Ford Fiesta.

Within a week, Colin had taken Jess on a couple of test-drives in his car. A restaurant one night and then the movies two nights later.

Within a year, Colin and Jess were living together.

Within two years, they were married.

Within two more years they had their daughter.

No more children came along, and Colin and Jess dedicated their lives to their daughter growing up, moving up from a terraced house to a semi and then a detached property, with enough space for two cars. Jess became a Front-Line Nurse Manager in a large hospital some twenty miles away from home, while Colin became a manager of a car showroom thirty minutes away from home in the opposite direction.

Their house was empty for large portions of the day. Their daughter moved away after university, married the man that she fell in love with during her course and within three years had two boys. Colin and Jess doted on their grandchildren but found it difficult to see them that often as they were both very busy at work. Colin found himself at the showroom almost every day in the week, helping out in the showroom, to keep healthy profit lines for the business. Jess, on the other hand, was in popular demand – about once a month she gave lectures at universities around the country for prospective medical students and she was occasionally away at conferences. They became like ships in the night. Passing occasionally in different directions and with different destinations.

During those different journeys Jess met a doctor; they quickly became friends and then on their so-called conferences became secret lovers. When Colin late one night overheard a short, whispered phone conversation when Jess was locked away in the bathroom, the secret was out, and their marriage was over.

After the divorce, and the halving of assets, Colin threw himself into the management of the showroom. He lived a quiet life, particularly in the evenings. He was tired when he got home from work. He made himself some food, watched some television and went to bed.

His daughter would phone him up twice a week as she did her mother, trying to be fair to her parents. She admitted to Colin that although she knew that her mother was in the wrong, she could not stop loving her mom and wanting to speak to her each week. Colin accepted that this was how it was going to be.

He also accepted it, when Jess married the rich doctor and saw pictures of the wedding and honeymoon in The Maldives. Her daughter and family attended. Her family, all but her dad.

As happens in life, Colin woke up one morning and questioned his life. He was beyond a mid-life crisis; it was more like a two-thirds of the way assessment. He didn't know how many more MOTs he would pass. He didn't know when the engine would seize up or when the petrol would run out, but he was not going to carry on along the same road.

Colin kick-started his life. He cut back on his hours at work and let his deputy take more of the strain. He bought a small, detached house – three bedrooms and a bit of a garden. He spent the weekends DIYing and gardening and attended the odd football match or concert. He joined the gym and attended quiz nights at the local pub.

When he looked in the mirror now, he was happier than he had been for a while. But he still felt lonely. He felt jealous of his ex-wife and his daughter who both had partners. A special person to come home to at night. Colin didn't have that. He didn't have a special someone to go with him to the theatre, the football match, the quiz night at the pub or just to share a meal in a restaurant or at home.

So, Colin joined Meet My Match and crossed his fingers that some woman out there would 'befriend' him or at the very least, take pity on him.

He bought some new smart and semi-smart clothes and prepared for a date. He wasn't sure of the protocols of dating sites, but people had warned him that it was not a smooth and easy process. He found that out quickly over a month when the first three female friends that he identified as potential matches did not materialise at the neutral meeting place. 'Were they real?', 'Was it a joke by someone?' or 'Am I not a catch?' Colin despaired but valiantly pledged to continue his search as he had paid for six months on the dating site.

Two weeks later, he landed his first catch. A nice enough woman who was very quiet but after a couple of hours received a phone call and claimed that she had to leave because her friend had been taken to hospital. Colin knew a phoney storyline when he heard it, having sold cars for a living for most of his life. He was quite relieved when she left the pub though, as he managed to watch the big match on the pub's large wide screen TV.

A week later, at the same pub, Colin met a very attractive woman, who looked better than her photo on the site. She was bubbly and quite forward. Colin thought that this lady could be the one to enjoy some nights out with. Unfortunately, she seemed only interested in his house and the distance it was from where she lived. As the night enfolded it became clear that she wanted some extra-marital enjoyment away from staring eyes on a week-to- basis. Out of courtesy, Colin took her details and left the pub before the final whistle. He did not want such an arrangement. That solution would not solve his loneliness and emptiness.

By the time Maureen and he exchanged messages, Colin was quite guarded. He had lost faith in Meet My Match and was into his fourth month. He kept Maureen at arm's length. Not that she was too eager herself, but he wanted to proceed slowly and find out a lot more about the person before they met.

The clock was ticking on his six-month subscription when he asked Maureen if she was prepared to meet him. She lay down the ground rules - he would pick her up from her front door, they would share a meal and he would drop her home.

At 7.58 pm, Colin sent Maureen a text.

I'm outside your front door. I hope you open it when I ring the bell.

Part Three

Maureen sat on the bottom of the stairs looking at the back of the front door. She had her mobile phone in her hand.

Colin walked slowly back to his car and sat in the driver's seat for a minute or two. His phoned pinged.

Thank you for a lovely evening. You were a real gentleman and friend listening to me babbling on all night. Also, thanks for sticking to the rules!
It was a pleasure. I really enjoyed your company.
I wasn't expecting you to answer my text until you arrived home.
I'm still outside your house.
I don't suppose you'd like a drink before you drive home.
A cup of tea or coffee would be great.
You could always have something stronger.
I'm worried about being over the limit if I have any more wine. The manager of a car showroom with a driving ban is not a good look!
Then don't drive home tonight. I'm opening the door now.

GHOSTWRITER

It's weird. If I told anyone at work that I'm a ghostwriter, they would inevitably jump to the conclusion that I'm a writer of ghost stories like Henry James or Susan Hill. Not that any of them would know about those particular authors. Up until recently I have been working alongside other shelf stackers at the local DIY superstore. The minimum wage isn't enough to pay the mortgage, but I manage for now. As a special treat from time to time, I buy some make-up to cheer myself up by hiding behind a false mask. Not that I go out much these days. I am either in the superstore working, in my bed sleeping or tapping away on this laptop.

Shelf stacker turned ghostwriter – that's me. I promise you - I don't write ghost stories. To be honest with you, I don't even believe in the supernatural. I'm not interested in ghouls or gods. The only god I believe in is the money god. The god of plenty that's supposed to fund your dreams.

It wasn't always like this. Ten years ago, when I started university, I was sure that one day I was destined to be a well-known and successful writer. I had aced my A levels and my English teachers all through my secondary and further education raved about my diction, my style and my creative imagination. So, off I went to Birmingham University to study 19th and 20th Century Literature, deluding myself that one day when students studied 21st Century writers, my name would be on the required reading list.

I must admit that I really enjoyed my time at university. I learnt a lot about the great poets, playwrights and novelists of the last two hundred years. I carried on where I left off at school by achieving impressive grades and receiving encouraging praise from my tutors. I also had a good time with my study group. There were eight of us. Looking back, we were all a bit serious and sensible compared to many of the students who seemed to spend far too much time playing drinking games in the union bar and not enough time studying.

Don't get me wrong, I wasn't a complete geek or prude, I liked to party as much as the next person, but I wasn't going to end up with a class A drug addiction at the expense of a first-class degree. It seemed that all of my study group felt the same way. We enjoyed reading and analysing literature and we loved to talk about novels, plays and poetry. A couple of times in the week we would meet up in someone's flat and we'd chat about what we were reading and sometimes we'd tell each other about our own attempts at writing. It sounds nerdy but it wasn't that serious, in fact it was quite a laugh as we would take the piss out of each other's supposed masterpieces. The funniest member of the group was Ian. He was an excellent writer; he was good company and he had a wicked sense of humour. Ian had a deep voice that was easy on the ears and his rugged appearance was not too bad on the eyes, either. Although the study group continued for the whole first year at university, Ian and I would often spend other evenings studying together in either his room or mine. We became close and then very close. By the end of the first year, we became an inseparable couple and studying took a back seat and the bed became the most important piece of furniture in our rooms.

In the second year at university, two separate rooms became one, and we played at being grown-ups, by sharing rent, cooking and cleaning and consequently at some point in our relationship we fell out of lust and into love.

Our single-mindedness at getting Firsts was distracted and derailed a little by our love and passion for each other rather than the books we were studying. By the final year of university neither of us seemed to have a clear career plan. I thought I might teach English or try to work for a publisher, but Ian did not want to work for any sort of company and he was not that keen on the prospect of teaching children. All he wanted to do was write. He was an outstanding writer and had won a few awards for the short stories he'd entered in competitions over the last couple of years. He had a style all of his own, an entertaining and engaging way with words and an ingenious way of structuring his writing. I know I was biased but I was convinced that he would have a future as a writer. When we left university, Ian had the first draft of a novel on his laptop. It was a best-seller in the making.

We pooled our resources and rented a two-bedroom flat in Tamworth. I went to work full-time in an advertising company some distance away from the flat. I wrote meaningless captions and blurb for products I didn't care about. It was hardly James Joyce or Earnest Hemmingway. Our agreement was that Ian would stay at home and spend six months re-writing his novel until he thought it was ready to be published. If he wasn't successful getting the book published, then he would also find a paid job.

After eight months or so, Ian sent off some sample chapters to various publishing companies, expecting a series of rejections by email. But within three weeks a publisher took up his novel and offered him an option of a three-book deal if his first novel made money. The first cheque he received went towards a deposit for our first house – an old-fashioned detached property on three levels on the old side of town. Three bedrooms, two reception rooms, a study, a wine cellar and a reasonable sized back garden. A home for children, a comfortable lifestyle and new exciting chapters.

I carried on writing meaningless copy at the office in town while Ian started his second book. I began to hate the job, but it meant that my wages could keep us going until the second book was published. The publishers wanted it finished within a year. Unfortunately, this became an issue for Ian. He couldn't cope with the pressure, he struggled with the ideas, the characters and the sequencing of the storyline. He became frustrated at his progress and there were days when I came home at night and nothing of value had been saved on his laptop. I tried to support him and sympathise with him but there were times when he became so grumpy and self-absorbed that he wouldn't even ask me about my day. On good days he let me read some of his writing and occasionally he'd let me suggest improvements, although I never referred to them in this way.

After a real struggle he sent off a draft of his second novel. I thought it was good (not in the same league as his first book, but still a great read) but the copy editors at the publishers pulled it to pieces and it took Ian another six months before they were satisfied with it. The book came out and it had a mixed reception, and some critics were quite hard on it.

We were still relatively young but by this time in our lives we were both shattered physically and emotionally. I was working hard at the office, keeping the house and garden clean and tidy, often cooking meals while Ian sat in his study moaning about losing his inspiration, writer's block and jacking it all in. He would say some thoughtless things to me like that he hated being cooped up all day and that he felt stifled. He wanted to get away, have a change of scenery, reinvent himself. He admitted one night that he needed a break from writing and from me.

14

What Ian said to me was hurtful, but I didn't take it too seriously as I believed that his anger and frustration were not really aimed at me but on the fact that he couldn't think of a good idea for his third novel. I suppose it must have been about a month later that I came back from work one night and discovered a note on the kitchen table. The note simply said:

I'm taking a break. I'll be in touch. Ian x.

That was all he wrote. The shortest story Ian had ever written.

He took nothing with him. On one hand it was a hopeful sign that he would return home soon. Most of his clothes remained in the house and significantly he left behind the laptop he used.

After several weeks of sadness, anger and despair, I came to the conclusion that Ian wouldn't be coming back home, not for a while at least. I kept myself busy in the house by decorating a few rooms. When weeks turned into a few months I moved most of Ian's stuff into the basement including his writing desk. I didn't want constant reminders of the man who had broken my heart. I kept his laptop in the living room, but I didn't look at it very often. I just deleted his junk mail from time to time.

Some nights when I couldn't sleep, I would look at my phone, to see if Ian had sent me a text or email. Nothing. He had disappeared from view. Where was he? Was he still alive? I didn't know if I should contact the police, but I decided to wait, as I was sure he was going to come back any day soon.

To keep myself busy in the evenings I decided to start writing again. I felt it would be cathartic for me if I could write something down. I used Ian's laptop. Within a few weeks I had an idea for a piece of writing about hope, ambition, love and betrayal.

Strangely, I started to enjoy writing again. It gave me some joy in my miserable, lonely existence. They often say that the best writing comes from the worst moments in someone's life. I have to admit that I was quite pleased with the writing that poured out of my heart and on to the screen. Maybe I could live without Ian. Maybe, sometime soon, I could reinvent myself and go on a dating site. God knows, I needed someone in my life again. I couldn't just live in this house with the ghost of my one and only true love.

One night, when I opened Ian's laptop to continue my writing, I checked his emails. There was a message sitting in his inbox from his publishers. They were asking for an update on his third book. How were things going? Was he still on track to meet the deadline? When could they see a synopsis? When could they see some draft chapters?

Panic ensued. I couldn't contact Ian to tell him about the need to get his third book ready. I couldn't contact the publisher and tell them that my boyfriend had left me and was no longer writing in case he was on a desert island somewhere completing the last chapter of his third book. What was I to do?

Well, I suppose you have guessed what I did by now. In the next few days, I quit my full-time job at the advertising company and found a part-time position in a home improvement store and began my other job as a ghostwriter. I wrote back to the chief editor, as Ian, and told her that I was some way though the next book and I would send her a synopsis soon with the first few chapters. I explained that I was laying low and was trying to stay away from distractions and only wanted contact through emails. The publishers accepted this, which gave me (and Ian) some breathing space. If Ian came home, I could tell him what the situation was, or I could come up with an idea for a novel that I could pretend he was writing.

Unfortunately, Ian was a no-show and in desperation I decided to write something that would fool the publishers. I spent a week trying to come up with an idea for the novel, but nothing seemed right. I couldn't copy Ian's style or his composition. After a fortnight of burning the midnight oil, I reluctantly conceded that Ian would lose out on the most lucrative last part of his three-book deal. Ian and I were scuppered.

One night, I sat at Ian's laptop and decided to confess to his publishers that he was missing in inaction and a book wasn't going to b produced. Just as I was going to send the confession, I came up with an alternative plan of action. I would send off my ideas and the first three draft chapters that I had been writing recently. I anonymised the pages and told the editor that I had decided to write the third novel with a new voice and style following the criticisms of my second book.

I had a response from the editor a week later saying that although it was quite a different novel and that some of the readership may not like the new style there was a possibility that this change may work. They wanted more chapters in the next month and the first draft finished in three months.

Emotions ran wild. I could become a published writer. They liked my writing. I had a future in something other than climbing the greasy pole in retail. I could be rich. I could be famous. And then of course it hit me. It wasn't me. None of this could be me. I was Ian. I was a shelf stacker. He was the writer. And without his name on the front cover, the book would never be published.

After a few days of arguing with myself and holding crisis talks with my conscience, we agreed that I should continue with the subterfuge. If nothing else, I would finish the book, abide by the publisher's comments and criticisms and head towards the finishing line before I had to admit that Ian had not written the book. So, I locked my conscience in the cupboard under the stairs and spent every waking minute finishing my book (or should I say Ian's book?) I put all thoughts of joining a dating site to one side. I was a fully committed ghostwriter. The only time I was actually myself was when I was walking up and down the aisles of the superstore. The rest of the time I was Ian. Ian, the writer. Ian, the man who ghosted me. Ian, the ghost in our own house. It was a bizarre experience.

In reality, I hated Ian. I hated him for walking away and leaving me to fend for myself. He was a self-absorbed, selfish bastard. He clearly didn't love me anymore. I hadn't received any sort of message for eight months now and with everything happening in my false life, I was hoping that he would stay away and never return. If nothing else, I knew now that I could write and I knew I could find someone out there to share my life in the future. Someone I could trust, someone honest.

Of course, things didn't work out as smoothly as I had hoped. The publishers liked the manuscript, and I dutifully made all the alterations that they wanted without any quibbles. When they asked for a new publicity photo for the back cover, I sent them a selection of photographs I had taken of Ian from my phone in the six months or so before he disappeared. They were satisfied that they could use one of them. They also talked about a book signing tour and I emailed them back saying that if the book came out just before Christmas, they could book me in for some slots for the new year.

I thought I had covered my tracks until a new message appeared on Ian's laptop. It was from Ian.

Hi,

Sorry I've not been in touch before now. I hope you're well. I realise you may not want to see me but I feel I owe it to you to give my side of the story. I don't expect you to forgive me but I hope we can come to some sort of understanding. So much has happened to me since I left and I believe I've now found peace and happiness at last. I'm in the area in a couple of days' time and I intend to come by the house. If you've moved on, so be it, but it would be good to see each other once more.

Ian x

After I read the email for the twenty-third time, I cried and shouted abuse at the laptop. This was my laptop now, not his. So, the bastard was feeling a slight pang of guilt. He wanted to drop in to get my blessing for walking out on me. He wanted to tell me all about his new life with, I assume, a new partner and a new career. Somehow, in his deluded state of mind he wished to absolve himself of any blame because now he was happy and at peace. And he just hoped that I was well. As in - not sick!

My mind was in turmoil for an hour or so before I made the decision to not open the door when he dropped by. I didn't want to see him. I didn't want to speak to him. What if he brought his new supermodel girlfriend with him? No way was I going to open the door to him. But did he still have a key? Maybe I should go out all evening for the next few nights so even if he could get in the house, I wouldn't be there. But did I want him in the house without me being there?

Three hours later I changed my mind. I would open the door and let him in. I would listen to his story and then I would start a new chapter of my life.

Two nights later there was a knock on the door. I invited Ian into my house. He was on his own. I made him a coffee and he talked to me for an hour or so about his travels and adventures around various countries, his short-term jobs working in bars or grape picking or whatever. He said he liked the open road. The freedom. The independence. The lack of responsibility. He saw it as a gap year that would probably last for two or three more years. Then he would settle down somewhere, write up his experiences as a travel log and get it published. He showed me his one precious possession, a folder he had stuffed in his backpack which was crammed with mementos from touring. He thought I would be interested. Not once did he ask about me, about his three-book deal or the mortgage on the house. It was only after another half an hour or so that I managed to shut him up. That was when I gave him a second and last mug of coffee.

It took me half the night to drag Ian's dead body down into the basement. I left it a day or two before I systematically started to dispose of Ian, his writing desk, and the folder of his travels (he wouldn't need to refer to that again). It was quite handy that my superstore sold all of the items I needed in order to wipe the slate clean and to keep the basement smelling fresh.

Several weeks later I wrote an email to the publisher as Ian, admitting that he had not written the third novel. 'Ian' explained that a friend had written it and she would be happy for the book to still to be credited to him but that she should get the profits from the sales of the novel. At the end of the email 'Ian' supplied the publisher with my name and contact details and told them that he would not be in contact again as he no longer wanted to be a novelist or in the public eye. Finally, I attached the finished draft of the novel and pressed Enter. With that I closed all contact between Ian and the publisher.

My own contact with Ian finished a few weeks later. I had quit working at the superstore and booked a short break away at the coast. I hired a small boat and each day headed out to sea to quietly dispose of the bleached bones and the remains of his broken laptop.

In the new year Ian's new book was launched. The mystery writer didn't appear at the launch or at book signings. The story went that he had become a recluse and would not be seen in public again.

Unlike Ian, I was happy to meet with the publishers on various occasions to discuss the new books I would write for them. I was also wined and dined by one or two rather attractive men at the top of the organisation. Perhaps there would be a happy ending somewhere in my future.

But, for now, I live and work in my happy place. My house. The home I share with Ian. I'm not sure I can ever leave him and he can never really leave me as he's my inspiration to be a real writer.

CLOSE

Part One

Stephen

I don't know why I chose to study History at GCSE. I didn't really like it in primary school or in Years 7, 8 and 9, but I had no choice. Well, actually I did. I had to choose one of the Humanities' subjects and it was either History, Geography or Religious Education. In the end it was a case of which subject did I hate the least. So I ended up in Miss Phillips' History class. Three hours a week. Making notes on wars, kings and queens. Looking at worksheets, pretending to listen to the teacher droning on. To say it was boring was an understatement. I don't want to give you the impression that I hated all of my subjects at school. I didn't mind Maths and I really liked IT, Science and Sports but I didn't like the lessons when you had to do a lot of writing – particularly English and History.

I started to enjoy History lessons in Year 10, though. It was not the teacher – Miss Phillips was OK – but nothing dynamic. It was the other pupils in the class that made it fun – two in particular.

Miss Phillips had a seating plan for us the first time we entered her room. When it was my turn to be 'seated' she told me to sit by Nick Leigh. The double table was two thirds of the way back on the left-hand side by the windows. This suited me fine. I liked Nick, he wasn't a close school friend, but he was a good laugh and he had the same attitude towards History that I did. The benefit of sitting by the window was also that the classroom overlooked one of the football pitches, so when the History lesson became boring, as it inevitably did, I could watch a game of football.

After the first week of lessons in September, the weather got particularly warm and sitting by the windows in the History lesson was almost uncomfortably hot.

On the fourth History lesson Miss Phillips announced that we could take our blazers off. Nick and I were quick to take our blazers off and hang them on the backs of our chairs. The two girls in front of us left their blazers on for some reason.

20

Ten minutes into the lesson, the girl in front of Nick took her blazer off but the girl in front of me left hers on. I didn't know the girls' names. I had never been in a lesson with either of them before. They were probably very intelligent girls who were in the top sets for everything – unlike Nick and me. This class was a mixed-ability class which included swats and dummies!

Ten minutes later the unknown girl in front of me succumbed to the heat and took her blazer off. She looked back as she hooked her coat on her chair and briefly smiled at me before swivelling round to listen to Miss Phillips.

It was at that moment – at 12.20pm on Monday 11th September that I fell in love. This girl had a beautiful face, smile and dark brown eyes that matched her long, curled hair. I was smitten.

I have to admit that for the rest of the lesson my eyes were directed at the girl in front of me, not the middle-aged teacher trying to enthuse the class about some sort of treaty.

This girl's long hair covered parts of her back but I was fascinated to see that her white shirt could not hide her dark-coloured bra. Please don't judge me too harshly, I was fourteen, almost fifteen, and any glimpse of the opposite sex's underwear was exciting and memorable.

It was day one of the rest of my life.

Miriam

I love History. I always have. I'm fascinated by understanding how the world evolved and developed. Humans are such complex beings. Over the centuries we have demonstrated that we are the most intelligent species living on the planet but also how stupid we can be. Our intellect has made us greedy, selfish and arrogant. We have lacked care and compassion for each other. But maybe, if we study the mistakes from the past, then we can create a better world for everybody. Particularly if women have more of a say in how things should be!

I really got my love of History in Year 7. The teacher I had that year, Mrs Harby, was amazing. She brought the subject to life. I had her again in Year 9 and I hoped I'd get her again in my GCSE years. But it was not to be. I had Miss Phillips. She's OK, but not as inspiring as Mrs Harby. Perhaps I'll have Mrs Harby when I study History at A level?

Then, when I become a teacher of History in about eight years' time, I will model myself on Mrs Harby, definitely not Miss Phillips. But for now, I'll keep my head down, study hard and take my time completing my essays.

Some of the others in my History class are not quite as motivated as I am. This is only the second week of the GCSE course but looking around the classroom there seems to be about two or three in the class who don't seem that interested. It's not that they have misbehaved, but they just don't seem to be all that keen on History. I can't help wondering why they chose to study the subject in the first place.

Anyway, I sat by Fiona, who was not only one of my best friends but also a hard worker. We hit it off from the day we started at secondary school together. We sat next to each other in tutor group and from then on, if we could, we would sit next to each other in every lesson throughout Years 7, 8 and 9.

So, when it came to Miss Phillips' class in Year 10, we naturally sat next to each other by the window. We were just over halfway back in the room with a couple of tables behind us. It felt like a good place to sit until the sun shone early on our fourth History lesson. It was really hot by midday and Miss Phillips told us that we could take our blazers off. Some of the class took their blazers off straight away. Fiona and I left ours on, but eventually we followed suit. Fiona took her blazer off first. I was sweltering in mine, but I was reluctant to take mine off. It was not in my thinking to even unbutton my blazer today. We did not have PE or Games today so why would I? But it was so hot. I had to take it off, but this was not what I wanted to do. My mother had washed my white bras and knickers on Sunday but she had forgotten to put the tumble drier on and so I had to wear some dark underwear to school. It wouldn't matter normally but I was self-conscious of displaying a black bra under a white shirt. It looked a bit tarty.

As I reluctantly took my blazer off and hung it on the back of my chair, I was aware of the boy behind me. I had never spoken to him in my life, but I had seen him around school. As I turned round, he smiled at me and I instinctively smiled back. I felt my cheeks starting to heat up. I felt uncomfortable. Did he think I was a tart for wearing a black bra to school? He gave me a lovely smile – what was that all about? I couldn't stop thinking about that moment. For the rest of the lesson, I couldn't concentrate on History.

From that History lesson onwards, I thought more about the present and the future, than I did about the past.

Part Two

Stephen

I looked into Miri's eyes. I looked at her radiant face. Her slightly red cheeks. Then I looked at her stunning white dress and smiled.

I whispered in front of the congregation, "No black bra?"

"You wish!" she whispered back with a cheeky smile.

In a minute or so I would be saying "I do." But while the celebrant goes through the initial part of the wedding ceremony, I am happy to look at my beautiful bride and remember some of the magical moments and milestones since we smiled at each other for the first time in Miss Phillips' History class.

I have to thank Miss Phillips for bringing us together in a way. The next lesson after we first smiled at each other, the teacher set a task which involved group work. We had to work in fours. The girls in front were told to move their chairs out of the way, push their table into ours and sit opposite us. Nick and I helped the re-arrangement and before long we had introduced ourselves and started working on the set task. Nick and I behaved ourselves and took the work seriously but managed to get the girls laughing with our daft teenage banter.

As it sometimes happens, once you speak to someone that you haven't spoken to before, you then keep bumping into each other and you have a chat. I would say hello to Miriam in the corridor, in the dinner queue, in the playground and at the bus stop outside the school gates.

It wasn't too long before we regarded each other as friends and would sit next to each other on the bus journey home. Miriam would get off one stop before me. In the mornings I would save a seat for her, next to me.

In History classes I would occasionally find a reason to touch her on the shoulder and ask her for a pencil or pen – just so that she would turn around and give me one of her smiles.

When it came to the last few months in Year 11, we would go to the school library once or twice a week where Miriam would help me with my History revision.

I did surprisingly well in my GCSE exams. I even got a fairly decent grade in History. Of course, none of my grades were as good as Miriam's but I did decide to stay on in the sixth form to study Maths, Physics and IT.

Miriam chose different subjects – English Literature, Psychology and, of course, History. This meant that we didn't see each other much at school. But we started to make up for that by seeing each other outside school. We would call in at one another's houses in the evening and go for a walk or go to a café and at weekends we would go shopping or the cinema. I can't remember exactly when I first held Miriam's hand or which film we were supposed to be watching when I reached over and kissed her on the cheek, but I do remember that when I walked her back to her house that night, we shared a goodnight kiss on her doorstep that lasted long in the memory.

For the rest of our time in the sixth form we were stuck like glue to each other. We were hardly ever apart in our spare time and when we were apart, we were texting or chatting to each other on our mobiles.

Perhaps because of our close relationship, our studying suffered a little, but we still managed to get into our preferred universities. I got into Aston University while Miri was accepted at Birmingham. Perhaps, not by luck but more by design, our unis were only a few miles apart. It meant that we could see each other quite often at nights and at weekends one of us would stay over at the other's digs.

After my three-year degree course studying IT, I secured a decent computer programming job in the middle of Birmingham. I rented a flat in Edgbaston so that I could be close to Miri.

Miriam stayed on another year to complete her PGCE. She then got a job teaching History, surprise, surprise, in a large secondary school close to my flat. She moved in with me and we decided to pool our resources and buy a house together.

That was some five years ago. By then we were both getting broody and so one night, after a meal out at a favourite local restaurant of ours, I popped the question.

So here we are on our wedding day and I'm about to say, "I do."

Miriam

Only Steve could make a joke about me wearing a black bra under my wedding dress in front of the celebrant and our families and friends. But that's what I love about him. That's what I loved about him after the first term in Year 10. Not only was he funny, but he was caring and not-bad-looking.

He looked great today. A new dark suit, his hair trimmed and a beaming smile on his face. That was the first thing I noticed about him in Miss Phillips' class all those years ago. Later on, in History lessons, when we sat opposite each other, I noticed that his smile moved up to his deep blue eyes. It didn't take me too long to be transfixed by him although I tried to play it cool for a while. When I say "a while" it was a couple of years before our friendship really developed into something serious. I had dated a lad in year 9 and fallen head over heels for him. Then he dumped me for another girl in my tutor group and after that I had stayed clear of getting close with another boy while my heart slowly mended.

So, I took my time, perhaps I took too long, because by the time we were in Year 11, we were more like good friends and study buddies rather than girlfriend and boyfriend.

But when we started sixth form, things changed. We weren't in any classes together, we didn't take the same subjects, so there was no reason to get together to study. But Steve still wanted to see me and I wanted to see him socially outside school. We'd go for walks, go shopping and go to the cinema most weeks.

I still remember the day that things really developed for the two of us. It was Saturday 5th October 2014. We were going to see "Gone Girl" at our local Cineworld. We dressed up to look over 18 and then decided to walk there. It was a cool evening and I had forgotten to take my gloves. When I started moaning about losing the feeling in my fingers, Steve took one of my hands in his and we walked to the cinema. When we sat down to watch the trailers, he took both of my hands in his and didn't let them go. Just as the film was about to start, Steve leant over to me. I was expecting him to whisper something daft in my ear but instead he took one of his hands off mine, turned my face round to meet his and then he kissed me on the cheek. He smiled. I smiled. Nothing was said. But within another minute or so he had kissed me again. This time on the lips. Needless to say, from then on, I found it difficult to follow the film. His arm found its way around my shoulders and the plot was punctuated regularly by kisses. It was lucky that no-one was sitting behind us because their view would have been severely restricted. The best kiss of all that night was when he said goodnight to me on my doorstep. Wow!

I know it sounds corny but from that movie night onwards, gone was the girl who just wanted a boy who was a friend. Now she was a young woman who wanted more than a friend and since that day I have never wanted to kiss another man in the way I kiss Steve, and I never will.

The years that followed seemed to speed by. We managed to go to universities in Birmingham that were relatively close together and so we continued to meet up in the evenings and at weekends and then during holidays we went home and saw each other practically every day.

Once I finished at university I moved in with Steve. We both had relatively good jobs for young twenty-somethings, and we agreed to save for a house ready for when children came along. We both wanted at least two little ones in our future.

One night we made the ultimate commitment. Steve asked me to marry him, and I said yes. We had gone for a meal at my favourite local restaurant. As usual, my hands were freezing when we got there, despite Steve holding one hand and then the other. When I started to moan about my fingers, he said he had just remembered that he had a pair of my gloves in his pocket. He gave them to me and told me to wear them until the meal arrived. When I stuck my left hand in my glove there was something inside the ring finger. It was an engagement ring.

And now and from this day forward, I will continue to love and care for Steve, for better, for worse, in sickness and in health. I do and I always will.

Part Three

Stephen

I've always liked watching Miri while she's asleep. It may seem a little creepy. But if I get up early and make us a mug of tea each, I will sometimes sit and watch her for a minute or so before I wake her up. I love to hear her content breathing and see the peaceful expression on her face. Occasionally there will be a trace of a smile on her lips. That smile soon evaporates when I wake her up and tell her that it is time to get up.

In our early days together, I would tell her to get up, so that we could both have a shower and eat breakfast together before we left for work.

A few years' later, it was just me having a shower and making breakfast while Miri fed the baby. Then, it was a slightly more complicated breakfast time when we had our second baby.

From then on, after I had the first shower, I would make breakfast for the family and prepare two lunch boxes, while Miri supervised the bathroom activities of the children after she was washed and dressed. We had two cars by this point in our grown-up lives. I would take the kids to school in one car and Miri would drive in the other direction to her secondary school where she was Head of the Humanities Department.

Eventually, there came a period in our lives when Saturday and Sunday mornings became the time in the week that we both longed for. Our teenage kids would be in bed until lunchtime, and we could sleep in, lie in and have breakfast in bed. It was bliss.

Somehow our children, in a blink of an eye, grew up into independent adults and fled their beds. Miri and I could, once more, just focus on ourselves in the morning. And I would revert to making Miri breakfast in bed and watch her sleeping for a short while.

Now, many years later, I get up early and in half an hour or so I am sitting close by her, watching her sleep. When she stirs, I help her take a drink and spoon feed her the meals that are prepared for her by the carers in the home. She sometimes recognises me. Sometimes she doesn't. But I love her, regardless. I love her more than ever. Our story began in Miss Phillips' History class in Year 10 many chapters ago. And I sit here and pray that there are still some pages left to be written in our history book.

Miriam

…Must get up…get dressed…shouldn't wear a black bra…get to school on time…History class…

…Drink of tea…thank you…man seems familiar…was he at school with me…pupil or teacher?.. he's sitting close to me…maybe he's a friend…

…It's getting late…must go…gone girl…

LIVING THE LIE

Working from home is still working. But not according to Beth's husband, Simon. His job was far more worthy and tiring because he had to work in a "proper" office after taking the train every morning and only to return home after six o'clock every night in order to earn his money. His wife on the other hand could sit at her desk in the spare bedroom, look at her laptop and talk on the phone without having a shower, combing her hair or changing out of her pyjamas. Beth knew that Simon's attitude to the way she worked was born out of resentment - he was just plain jealous. To add to his envy Beth earnt more than he did and was highly regarded by her boss and the board of her company – unlike Simon - who was regarded as the favourite whipping boy by his senior managers at work. Over the last few years Simon had also become aware that younger employees in the company were being promoted over his head.

Over time, Simon became more and more unhappy at work and with life in general. He became miserable, moody and agitated at home. He found it difficult to sleep at night and would often doze in his armchair when he finally got home after the 25-minute train journey and the 10-minute walk. About eighteen months ago Beth was so fed up with his state of mind and his lethargy that she insisted that Simon should talk to a professional about his mental health. His GP immediately wrote him a prescription for antidepressants. The medication made him sleep better during the night but unfortunately did not improve his attitude to work or life in general.

Beth found living with Simon more and more difficult. He would be snappy and sarcastic with her. He would be demanding and expect her to do all of the household chores because he was "too tired" or "stressed out." He would spend half of the evening asleep in his armchair which meant they would not get opportunities to talk like normal couples do. Beth desperately needed to talk to someone about her job, which she loved, but Simon wasn't interested or receptive. So, Beth talked to her friends on the phone in the evening or occasionally went out at night to have a chat while her husband slept in his armchair. She needed the company of real living people, not a zombie.

Beth and Simon were in their mid-fifties and yet most of the time she felt like an old lady looking after a semi-helpless patient. She would make their cups of tea. She would cook him his evening meal and do the dishes. She would be the one who vacuumed the house and dusted the surfaces. She would go shopping for food and general supplies. Beth did everything and Simon did nothing. She was at her wits' end. She couldn't face the rest of their working lives being like this. But no matter how many times Beth had tried to explain to her husband how she was feeling, the exchange would always end up with Simon insisting that if her life was hard then his life was even harder.

Week after week went by. If weekday evenings were bad, then the weekends were worse. Simon would lie in bed on Saturday and Sunday mornings feeling sorry for himself. And, if Beth didn't nag, he would sit in the armchair for the rest of the weekends watching sport on the TV or napping. Occasionally, he would go to the cinema with her to keep the peace, but he would often end up asleep through the second half of the film. After his incessant moaning about going for walks, going to restaurants with friends or joining a gym together, she gave up, admitted defeat and often left him alone in his armchair while she visited the park or a café with friends who she could talk to and feel like a fully-functioning human being.

Friday evenings were the worst. Simon was at his most tired and fed up after five consecutive days at work. He would come in just after six o'clock, take his coat off and plonk himself in front of the TV and expect a cup of tea to be placed on the table by the side of his armchair. There would be a very short conversation between the two of them before he dozed for half an hour, followed by his meal being served to him on a tray, before falling asleep again.

Beth decided that the next Friday evening would be different. Things would have to change.

When Friday arrived, Simon came home at 6.17 and performed his usual ritual of taking off his coat, placing it on the banister in the hall, kicking off his shoes, and slumping in his armchair.

"Hello, how was your journey? You're a bit later than usual," shouted Beth from the kitchen as she prepared Simon's cup of tea.

"Friday night rush hour is the worst. I hate the train. Too many people, not enough seats," replied Simon.

"Never mind love. It's the weekend now. You can relax," Beth said as she walked into the living room holding his cup and saucer in her hand. Simon hated mugs for tea. It had to be a china cup and saucer or nothing.

"Shall I draw the curtains and after you've drunk your tea you could catch forty winks while I make the meal? I need to pop to the shops for some ingredients while you have a nap.

"That's fine. I'll just have a sleep and then I'll have my meal, although I'm not that hungry."

"No problem," replied Beth. She closed the curtains and went back into the kitchen. She took a couple of 'bags for life' and headed out of the back door. She thoughtfully left the back door unlocked so that she could re-enter the house without disturbing Simon's sleep. She also took her time walking the long way round to the local Co-op.

It was over thirty minutes before she quietly opened the back door, crept through the kitchen and entered the dark living room. Beth surveyed the scene as best as she could in the half-light. Simon had drunk all of his tea. He was dead to the world.

"Simon. Wake up sleepy head. You told me to wake you after thirty minutes. Simon?" Beth touched Simon's shoulder. No response. Beth then shook his arm. Still no response.

Beth sat on the edge of the coffee table that was in front of Simon's chair. She glanced at the curtains to make sure they were closed. No-one could see into the living room even if they wanted to. She sat there and stared at her husband's head that was tilting to one side. It was too dark in the room to see his facial features, but she could not hear any snoring or breathing. The anti-depressants in the tea had done the trick. This was no longer a living room but a dead room.

"I'm so sorry about this, Simon. But I couldn't face another Friday night with you. Come to think about it, I couldn't face another weekend with you or another week. I know this isn't entirely your fault, but I couldn't carry on like this. I needed to change things. I wanted a new life. So, I've been making a few plans over the last month or two. Shall I tell you what I've done? Oh...sorry...you can't talk can you...or listen for that matter...so no change there then. But you will have to pretend to listen to me and hear my side of the story, even if you don't agree with it."

30

Beth stood up briefly, grabbed a cushion from her settee and sat back on the coffee table with the cushion making her feel a little more comfortable.

"You see Simon, I don't like you. I may have loved you many years ago but for the last ten years or so I haven't really liked you and, I'm sad to say, that I've grown to despise you."

"Why is that? I don't hear you say. Well, good question, Simon. It's probably because I've been living only in Simon's world. It's a very small world that consists primarily of one – you. There may be a few other people who enter and exit your world including me, but for the vast majority of the time you live on Planet Self. Your selfishness has crept up on me over the years and foolishly I didn't question it, I just accepted it…until now."

"It's not that you have been having affairs or gambling all of our money away. You have never hit me or really shouted at me. Strangely, it's worse than that. You just don't acknowledge me. You just forget that I exist."

"Over the last few months, I've been trying to work out how it ever came to this. I'm a reasonably intelligent woman. People generally like me. My work colleagues respect me. My friends say that I'm good company. I can still look good for my age. And yet to you, I'm invisible. So, was this all my fault? Did I let this happen to myself? Am I just a weak and pathetic wife? No, I won't accept that. You're to blame. Yes…you…not me. You are a bullying bastard. And now that you're gone, I won't lose any sleep because I can begin to enjoy my life again."

"So, while you're sat here, I'll tell you how I'm going to start my new life. Well, first of all, I won't be going to prison. Oh no! You see you committed suicide. You had enough. They treated you badly at work. Your doctor diagnosed your depressive state and gave you medication to try to make you feel better. But that didn't work. I told all of my friends that you were at the end of your tether, and you were having very dark days. You were at your worst on a Friday evening. Over the last few weeks, I've mentioned to my friends that I leave the house as soon as you get home from work. I don't even make you a cup of tea on a Friday night. I give you some space and go to the shops for a while. I would leave and return by the back door. By the time I got back you'd be peacefully dozing in front of the TV. And I would make the meal. Sometimes you'd make yourself a cup of tea before you go to sleep, sometimes you can't even be bothered to boil the kettle. And this has

31

been the way you've behaved on a Friday night for the last three months or so. Usually, by Saturday morning you're in a slightly better and more positive mood with the weekend ahead of you."

"And in my statement to the police this is what I will say to them…'when my husband came home from work, I left to go shopping to give him some time to relax. To my shock and horror, when I returned at just before 7.00 there was Simon lifeless in his armchair with an empty cup of tea by the side of him. I tried to wake him, but I couldn't. I didn't know what to do other than phone an ambulance.' The paramedics believed that he had taken a fatal overdose of his antidepressants, crushed up in his tea. The police will not find a suicide note but believe it to be a pre-determined deliberate act. I will look mortified. I will cry. I will sob. And there and then I will become a widow."

"So what will happen to me now? Of course, I will grieve, have the funeral and then grieve some more. I will be supported by my friends and then after a few months I will announce that I need to reinvent my life and enjoy myself, just as Simon would have wanted."

"My friends will encourage me to go on a dating site and after a few unsuccessful dates I will tell my friends that I have met a man called Geoff. Geoff and I will hit it off straight away. It will be as if we have known each other for some time. Maybe we have already! And within a year we will decide to live together and start a new life."

"So that's how it's going to be. I will ring 999 and tell Emergency Services that I have just got home from the shops and discovered you…lifeless.

And then I can start my new…"

Beth heard a key in the door. Then the front door slammed closed. Simon walked in. Beth looked at the clock on the living room wall. It was 6.17.

"What are you doing sitting in the dark? Sitting on that coffee table? What's got into you?" said Simon.

"Oh, nothing really…do you want a cup of tea?" replied Beth with a dark smile on her lips.

DANCING IN THE DARK

Dane

To many, this would seem like a glamorous lifestyle. Dancing and singing for a living. Audiences cheering and applauding after every performance. A rolling six-monthly contract with every chance it will be offered again if you are half-decent.

But with only a couple of months to go before my first contract is at an end, I have to decide if I want to do this again. Can I take the repetitive nature of the job with the boredom and frustration that goes with it, for another six months? Or shall I risk going back to the uncertainty of life on dry land?

My name is Daniel Worthington but to most of my family and friends in Birmingham I am known as Dan. My fellow dancers and singers on board The Majestic cruise ship call me Dane. Apparently, it sounds better. More exotic. I was also told when I joined the entertainment team on the ship that I should try to lose my Brummie accent and try to sound a little more sophisticated. This all might sound a bit like 'Billy Elliot' and I suppose, to some degree, it is.

I was born and raised in Erdington, north Birmingham, as far away from the sea as you can get. During my time at school, I always wanted to sing and dance rather than play football and cricket. At primary school I was chosen to play leading parts in the Christmas and end-of-year concerts. Everybody at school seemed to accept me as an 'arty pupil.' At secondary school some of the alpha males thought I was a 'bit gay' but I mostly got along fine with them all and was encouraged by The Performing Arts department to develop my skills. At the end of Year 9 I was accepted at BOA (The Birmingham Ormiston Academy for Performing Arts) and prospered there until I finished after my A levels. I acted in plays, sang and danced in musicals, and dabbled in directing and choreography.

My parents encouraged and supported me through my degree years at Birmingham University where I studied the Media. After all that experience which improved my skills on stage and behind it, there was just the small problem of finding a job. It was easy to get parts in small-time local shows, but I could not land any big gigs in London or any other major UK city. I went for hundreds of auditions, but I never got the chance to perform on a 'big' stage. So, that takes me to eight or nine months ago when, in desperation, I applied and was offered a six-month contract with a cruise company.

Admittedly, it wasn't the West End, but it was reasonably well-paid and meant that I could give up paying rent on a flat and save some money while I was at sea.

I became a member of the Showstoppers Entertainment Team that was assigned to the ship, The Majestic. She sailed mostly from Southampton to the Norwegian Fjords or she did trips around the UK coastline. I was drafted into a team of twelve performers, four of which were lead singers, and I became one of the eight dancers who sang to back up the main vocalists.

I didn't find the entertainment schedule too onerous. We'd rehearsed the shows in a studio in Southampton for a couple of weeks before we even boarded the ship. We would perform for three of the seven nights, two shows a night, for about 45 minutes at a time with a break of two hours between shows. Other nights we wouldn't be needed to perform on the big stage as other entertainers such as magicians, comics and tribute acts were brought in to vary the entertainment offer. It was good to have some evenings off from performing on stage but that didn't mean our free time as performers was our own. We had to fulfil other duties during each cruise that kept us both busy and knackered. The ten of us had to take it in turns to host games on the deck or in some of the nightclub areas during some evenings; we had to supervise excursions each time the ship docked; and help the rest of the crew on 'change over' day when passengers disembarked, and new passengers were welcomed on the ship.

It was fun and tiring, but the team, on the whole, were a good laugh and were patient with me as I was the newbie. There seemed to be a bit of a hierarchy within the team. The singers were the A-listers in the team and the dancers were the supporting cast. The director and chief choreographer was the main singer and had had West End experience in the past and I suspect was paid a lot more than I was. But I wasn't complaining. It was a job, and we were appreciated by the passengers. In our own small way, we were stars on the ship. Mainly because there is a captive audience on board a cruise ship - passengers would recognise us, comment on the shows and make us feel important and valued.

As the weeks went by though, the order of events and the shows became predictable. It was not the case for the holidayers on board – to them it was all new and different and after a week they were replaced by another ship full of excited new passengers. To the crew it was the same ol' same ol' but we had to try our best to make it seem new and different. The only thing I really looked forward to were the shows and some of the dance routines.

During a 45-minute show I would be dancing with the other men, in formation sometimes, sometimes with different women in pairs and sometimes all of us in sequences. But every evening I would get to dance for a few minutes with one of the female dancers called Stephanie. It would brighten up each day (or should I say night) for me. She was a gorgeous dancer, and I loved the opportunity to dance with her on stage - be it modern or traditional dancing, ballet style or freestyle – she was amazing. She was also beautiful and had a lovely personality and a witty sense of humour.

Stephanie was on her second six-month contract, and I'd heard from her cabin mate that she was anxious to finish at the end of her second term as she had a boyfriend back home in Gloucester.

Over the months we had got on well as friends and I decided that if she was leaving in a months' time I would quit as well and try my luck back in London.

But I couldn't stop thinking about Stephanie. It may seem weird to you, but there are very few places on the body of a dance partner that you haven't touched in a professional way during the shows we perform. But the part of her body I longed to touch was her lips, in a kiss.

Stephanie

I knew it. I suspected this may happen, but I thought he would have the guts to tell me himself before being told by a friend of mine. My friend saw him in town with a woman a week or so ago. Then she texted me to say that she'd seen him and the same woman in a nightclub and that they were all over each other. So I texted him last night after the show and I received his reply this morning. "Sorry babe but I've found someone else. Can't wait for you forever. I should've told you before now"…blah blah blah

Yes, you should – you asshole. Was it too much to ask to get a phone call? I know it's been a while since I was back in Gloucester. Five months. But I told you then that at the end of this latest contract I would take some time off and we could plan for a future together.

35

He seemed OK with that, but he clearly wasn't. I wonder how long he has been cheating on me. We've talked on the phone once a week and there has never been a hint that he was seeing anyone else.

I've never looked seriously at another bloke since I started working for this cruise company almost a year ago. I've never wanted to. I've just got on with my job as a dancer. There's been the odd male comedian or singer who has tried it on with me as a one-night fling, but I just brushed them away. It would make it difficult to have a fling even if I wanted one as I share a two single bed cabin with another dancer, Belinda. And anyway, most of the entertainment team on the ship are either happily married or are gay.

Belinda was married and had no plans to return to the ship when her contract expired in a month's time. She and her husband were planning to start a family as she was approaching the Big 3-Oh!

So, what am I going to do? I was going to finish at the same time as Belinda. I was going back to my boyfriend, become engaged, get married, own a house, have two children and perhaps get a proper job when they were both at school. Those were my hopes and dreams until I had a text from my friend and then my ex-boyfriend this morning.

Now, with all of those plans sinking to the bottom of the North Sea as we sail towards a Norwegian fjord, I am considering staying on this ship, or another one, and carrying on dancing. After all, I have nothing better to do with my life.

If I did one or two more years of this I could save up, get enough for a deposit on a house, take out a mortgage and buy a little home of my own. I can make different plans then. I've got time on my side. I'm only twenty-five now. I'm pretty fit and healthy. Then when I finish dancing on cruise ships, I can hopefully find a man with his feet firmly on the ground and we can lay down roots together.

But can I stomach another six months or more of dancing on the water? I am not one of the leading lights in the cast. There are several women who have made it clear to me that they are the real stars of the show. I am just an extra pair of legs. I have asked the musical director if I can have just one song of my own to sing. But she said 'Maybe, one day' and left it at that. So, for now, I don't get to sing a solo and I just dance and look as if I'm happy about it.

However, it's tiring and wearing. The audience expects a free Broadway show each night and yet we get paid very little in comparison to performers singing and dancing in the capital city. And yet we do exactly the same. The lightning quick costume changes, the constant pretend smile on my face, the jumps, the swivels, the splits and the endless practising and rehearsals.

But the audiences onboard the ship get to see our shows for free as part of the holiday package. Some of the people watching us couldn't really care what we do. Half of the audience are well over 70 years of age and having just eaten a 15-course meal or buffet are sleeping it off as soon as the lights go down. I swear, some nights, as I'm dancing, I can hear snoring and farting from the audience rather than cheering or clapping. Then there's the perves in the front rows of the auditorium who spend the evening just staring up at our knickers or hoping to catch a glimpse of our boobs as we perform our dance routines. It's so difficult to stay positive and happy when you are not really appreciated for what you do.

No-one on board thinks I'm that important, just like back in Gloucester. I don't think I'm appreciated at sea or on land, for that matter.

The only people that make me laugh are my cabin mate, Belinda, and one of the new dancers called Dane. He's a good dancer, really fit and a good laugh. Some time ago I mentioned to Belinda that when Dane dances with me I feel different. I am not just going through the motions with him. He's a real dance partner, not like the other men I dance with who look straight through me and never connect.

Considering Dane's gay, he is a very convincing actor. I feel like a desirable woman when he holds me, turns me round or holds me in a lift.

But with Belinda leaving, and the dancer I have a connection with being more interested in men rather than me, there isn't much point in me staying on this ship at the end of next month.

I think I will leave. Do something else with my life. It's a pity. I love dancing, particularly with the right partner.

We're on stage in forty minutes. Two small dressing rooms. Just need to put my sequins on for the first number and then my makeup. The show must go on, I suppose.

What's going on? I'm looking at Belinda talking to Dane in the small gap between our changing rooms. They look quite serious, which is odd as they are usually very funny and smiley. Now Belinda is pointing at me, I'm sure she is. Oh God, has she told him about my asshole exboyfriend? Dane's going to tease me about it later on when we all have a drink together after the second show. I'm going to kill Belinda. Why did she do that?

Daniel and Stephanie

"Here's your drink, Steph."

"Thanks Dane. I could do with it. Difficult day."

"Yeah, I heard from Belinda. I'm so sorry. You deserve better than that. I promise I won't let on to anyone else."

"Thanks, but it's done now. I don't really care if anyone finds out what an idiot I've been."

"He's the idiot, not you!"

"Perhaps, but it's made me re-think things. I've decided to quit next month and get a job of some sort on dry land."

"But you love dancing. You're a brilliant dancer…I love dancing with you…"

"Thank you, that's a nice thing to say. And I love dancing with you…but…"

"But what?"

"Oh nothing…"

"I was thinking of doing one more six-month contract on The Majestic before reassessing what I want to do with my life. I can't see myself doing this forever. I want to get a job in a theatre somewhere. I want to find someone to share my life with. Get a house. Have a family."

"That's nice. Considering all that is wrong with the world at the moment, it's great to know that people are tolerant of two dads bringing up a child."

"Yes…what? Sorry…what do you mean?"

"You know, two dads raising a family. I wish you luck."

"Well thanks, but I was rather hoping to find a more traditional way of being a partner and a parent."

"Sorry, I don't follow."

"Do I need to tell you about the birds and the bees?"

"I think you need to. I'm struggling a bit here."

"Well, here we go. I'll try not to blind you with science. But I have to warn you that I wasn't very good at Science when I was at school. But I do know a bit about Chemistry."

"Dane, you're confusing me. Is this one of your jokes?"

"No, I'm being serious. Maybe more so than I usually am with you."

"Oh God, I don't like the sound of this. I hope you're not going to upset me anymore than I already am. I'm not in the best of spirits after my boyfriend dumped me today."

"No…no…I'm not trying to upset you. I would never do that, Steph. I just want to explain something to you. Before it's too late."

"And this has got something to do with chemistry? I don't understand, Dane."

"Yes. Chemistry. The chemistry between two people."

"Well clearly there was no chemistry between me and my ex-boyfriend or he would have waited for me."

"You're right…but I've been waiting for you. Waiting in the wings. I've loved talking to you and making you laugh. I've looked forward to dancing with you at every opportunity on board this ship. And when I hold you in a dance routine, I never want to let you go. That's true chemistry."

"I love dancing with you too. You're the best partner I've ever had. We do have chemistry on stage and we have some great times off stage too but…"

"But what?"

"But it's just for show. We are…different people…"

"Yes, we are. Funnily enough I've noticed. I'm a man and you're a woman…"

"Exactly, Dane. That's why we are great dance partners. It's all pretence when we dance romantically together in a waltz or a rumba or a tango. Nothing else."

"But I thought…"

"What did you think? That we could be a couple? How would that work?"

"Well, I was hoping that one night after a show we could practice a slow dance together. Just us, an empty stage, the lights down low. I would hold you in a tight embrace and I would whisper in your ear that I loved you. We would kiss and then continue dancing in the dark until daybreak."

"But…you're…"

"In love with you…Yes…Completely. I have never felt this way about any other woman before. I know I might sound as if I'm overstepping, but I believe you're my perfect partner on sea…and on land. Steph, I would love to spend the rest of my life with you, kissing you, holding you and dancing with you. Even after we have children and grandchildren of our own. Am I making myself clear?"

"Perfectly."

FALLEN WOMAN

I look up at the ceiling and want to be taken to a different place and time.

"Oh, that's good!"

But I'm being taken right here and right now by a man that I don't know or care about.

"That's it babe!"

I try to make all the right noises, but I can't get excited.

"Come on bitch!"

This is just a job. This is my living. This is my life.

"That's right. I'm gonna cum!"

This is all wrong. How did it come to this?

I left school after studying some "A" levels. My mum couldn't afford for me to go to university. She wanted me working to help pay the bills. So, I got a job in the offices at a local distribution centre. I would spend my days answering the phone and inputting data into various spreadsheets. It was boring but it was above the minimum wage. I had a bit of money left over each week to go out with a couple of girls I'd kept in touch with from school. We'd often get wasted on a Friday night at the local pub and if we could all afford it, we'd sometimes go from the pub into town to a nightclub. We were all single and ready to be pulled.

I had my fair share of boyfriends but none of them lasted very long. Nothing serious. Over time, though, my two friends got properly lovey-dovey coupled up and our boozy nights became a thing of the past.

I began to spend all my nights at home watching TV. Even my mum was having more fun than I was as she had hooked up with a new boyfriend who took her out about three nights a week. After a while he started to stay over at our place, and with the wall between mum's bedroom and mine being paper thin, I knew it was time to rent a flat of my own.

Luckily, I'd got a bit of a promotion at work and that meant I could rent a small flat and give the landlord a month's rent in advance and a deposit. The flat was OK. A living room and kitchen combined, a bathroom, one reasonable-sized bedroom and a very small bedroom that I used for storage. It didn't have much furniture in there, so over the next six months or so, I managed to get some second-hand kit that made the place more homely.

I was 24 years old; I had a place of my own and a reasonable job. I restarted my love-life by going on a few dating sites. On a scale of one-to-ten some of the blokes were at four or five, but most of them were one or below zero! A few of them were worthy of a night on my second-hand bed, but not many.

I saw less and less of my mum who was now starry-eyed with her new fella. She moved in with him and gave up her place. He was alright, I suppose, and he treated mum well, so I was pleased for her.

On my 25th birthday, the folks in the office held a little party for me after work. Even the boss came to wish me well and toasted me from a plastic cup full of cheap bubbles. It was the best birthday I had ever had. All my work colleagues were nice to me and I was the centre of attention for a few hours. I must admit, I got a little bit drunk on the fuss I was receiving and the bubbles I was drinking. One of the guys from the management office upstairs offered to take me home. He was older than me, but good-looking and funny, and after he drove me home, he helped me up the two flights of stairs to my flat. I invited him into the flat and we sat and had a coffee before we had semi-drunken sex on the second-hand settee. After that, I invited him to stay the night but to my surprise and disappointment he said he had to get home to his wife and kids.

That should have been the end of it. I was not one to break up a marriage or a family, so I put the episode behind me and pretended that the settee sex had not happened. Four days later, after I had caught a bus home from work, he was standing outside the flats where I lived, waiting for me. He came into the flat, drank coffee and apologised for his behaviour and asked for my forgiveness. We agreed that it was just a moment of weakness and that we would not talk about it again, to anyone.

Fifteen minutes later we were having sex on, in and around my bed. And an hour later we agreed again not to talk to anyone about this…again!

Again and again we made this agreement. He would come round to my flat as often as he could after phoning his wife with a believable excuse for being late home.

After many, many visits, I started to believe that he couldn't do without me. There were things that he said to me, in bed, that gave me the impression that he was going to leave his wife. I had hope. Hope of love and a normal family life. The two of us. A house of our own. Then a baby and then another one, after that. He would obviously still see his other children at weekends or in school holidays if he wanted to. As long as he knew where his real home was.

We started to talk about the future. I made it clear that I wanted to start a family soon. I wanted a baby, his baby, so badly. He started looking at our finances. He was due a promotion and a big raise in the next three months. Once he divorced his wife, he would have half of the house minus alimony payments. Our two salaries combined would mean that we could afford a small, terraced house on the other side of town. It may be tight for a while, but we could tighten our belts. After all, we were in love, and we could cope.

I came off the pill and very quickly I got pregnant. We were thrilled but we had to keep our excitement to ourselves. No-one at work could know…yet. Not until he split from his wife. He promised it would all be sorted in the next month or two before my belly grew too big.

By the end of my first trimester, I was wearing looser clothing. I loved being pregnant. I loved the thought of having a baby. But as my stomach grew, so did my anxieties. He kept promising me that he was waiting for the right time to tell his wife. When would this secret affair become general knowledge? When would it all be resolved?

A few days' later it was resolved. The father of my child came round after work one evening and broke the news that he was staying with his wife. She had found out somehow that he was having a "fling" and she had given him an ultimatum. The deal was that he would have to finish the affair immediately and she would allow him to stay in the house or, if he left, he would never see his children again. That's the story he told me, anyway. I didn't believe him for a second, but he had made up his mind – he was staying with his wife. And even worse, he wanted me to have an abortion.

I told him that that decision was mine, not his. Over the next week, while trying to go to work each day with a broken heart, I had to decide about my baby. I decided I would keep the baby. I'd have to get childcare somehow after my maternity leave finished, but I wanted my baby, even if the father did not want me.

In the next month, I noticed a change in the way people at work regarded me. I had the silent treatment from some of my colleagues, and others, who I was quite friendly with, became distant.

It felt like only a couple of weeks' later that I was informed by my boss that changes were being made in the department and my position was being absorbed into other people's job roles. In a word, I was being fired.

In a matter of weeks, I was on my own, six months' pregnant and out of work.

The next couple of years were a forgettable blur. Other than giving birth to my beautiful son, Ben. There was nothing in my life that was memorable. I never went out. No dates, no boyfriends. It cost me less to stay at home and look after my child than it was to work. So, I stayed in the flat. Trapped in a poverty trap. I had to use food banks and charity shops to get by, propped up by benefits.

But I couldn't survive like this for long. I needed extra money to give Ben a better life. I had fallen into the gutter, but I was damn sure Ben would not follow me.

So I made a plan. My heart may have been closed to love, other than for Ben, but my legs were open for business.

"Come on bitch, work for me."

There should be a better way to make money!

"I'm paying for the full works, baby. Get to it!"

God, this guy is so noisy. I hope he doesn't wake up Ben in the next room.

"Harder, harder. I want my money's worth. Use your hand!"

And I want my money's worth. And I'll get it, after I send him the video of this little fling with me. Then he'll be paying me a large bonus to keep this footage away from his wife. A few of these flings a week will keep Ben and me afloat. I can work from home. I can set my own hours. No taxes to pay. Now that's what I call 'cash in hand.'

THE LEDGER STONE

I must confess…I rarely go to church…just weddings, christenings and funerals…mainly funerals these days!

But while I'm confessing, I suppose I ought to tell you that I have been known to enjoy wandering around graveyards. I like to walk around the graves, looking at the flowers or tributes placed carefully by loved ones at some of them. In particular, I have to admit, I am fascinated by the inscriptions that are chiselled on the headstones.

In one sense, the messages on the headstones are very personal and I feel as if I'm intruding by reading the inscriptions composed by living strangers to dead strangers. But I convince myself that I'm not over-stepping, as I only have a few snippets of information about these people's lives – their names, their immediate family left behind and the day of their births and deaths. I don't think I'm prying, I'm just interested in keeping memories of the dead alive. It may seem morbid. Perhaps it is, but I'm sure that I'm not the only person who has wandered around a graveyard feeling moved by the lives of children and adults captured in a few lines. I'm also certain that I'm not the only person who reads an inscription and tries to fill in some of the blanks from the three or four lines engraved on the cold, hard stone. I like to think that I'm not cold-hearted myself, but a fellow traveller who has not yet reached his final destination and has not, as yet, been able to make sense of life or death.

This brings me to the purpose of these few words I have written on cold, hard copy.

Last month my wife and I were visiting Gloucester. We were sight-seeing, taking photographs, spending money and ticking boxes from our tourist guidebook. The beautiful cathedral beckoned us; although neither of us are religious, we felt the need to have a look at the inside as well as the outside of this magnificent structure.

It was a crisp autumn day and in the October sunshine the outside of the cathedral looked majestic and when we stepped inside it was both atmospheric and evocative. The internal design was stunning, and the objet d'art was breath-taking. My eyes were constantly being drawn upwards to the delicate stained-glass windows portraying stories from the bible. There came a point where I just stood still mesmerised and marvelling at the colourful and intricate glass work, but when I looked down, I was horrified to see that I was standing on someone's grave.

I wasn't doing anything wrong. Parts of the cathedral consisted of ledger stones laid side by side and it was acceptable for visitors to walk on the stones. But when I considered it, I found it unnerving and disrespectful. It wasn't something I was used to. In all of my visits to graveyards over the years I had never consciously stepped on a grave. I would read headstones from six or seven feet away or from the side of the grave. But at this moment in Gloucester Cathedral, I was standing on a dead body admiring the view.

Clearly, I was not the only person to walk over these ledger stones. The rest of the visitors inside the cathedral seemed happy and guilt-free, even though they were walking on top of graves, taking photographs to show to their friends and family.

I, on the other hand, stood rooted to the spot. I felt the need to apologise to the dead person. So, I bent down to see who I should make my apologies to. This represented a problem for me because the one side of this particular ledger stone had been worn away by the many visitors to the cathedral over the centuries.

I couldn't make out very much of the inscription, so I took a photograph of the ledger stone in order to research the person at a later date.

Back at our hotel, I looked again at what was left of the ledger stone's inscription. This is all that I could decipher…

Here interred R
the Body of Brid
Wife of John Vau
Who departed this
The 14 day of
February Ao
1669
Resurgamus

My amateurish investigation started, and these were my initial findings and thoughts:

- A woman (Oh God! I stepped on a dead woman – sorry!)
- The date of her death – well over 400 years ago

- Married to a chap called John (sorry John for stepping on your wife)
- No real need to apologise to John, as he's clearly been dead for a while (I don't feel quite as bad now)
- From the Latin word Resurgamus, there was an intention to 'rise again' (Oh God! Not while we're all walking over her body every day! – sorry, again!)

That was as far as I could get. Google and Gloucester Cathedral's records could not give me any answers to questions like:

What was her first name? Was it Bridget?

What was her last name – her maiden and married name?

Is 'Vau' part of John's middle or last name?

When was she born, and therefore, how old was she when she died?

What was the cause of her death?

Where did they live?

Was John wealthy? Surely he was, if he could afford a grave inside Gloucester Cathedral?

Was she an important figure in Gloucester?

Did she have children?

But I couldn't answer any of these questions. I hadn't got the necessary information. But what I did have was years and years of experience of looking at gravestones and filling in the gaps and although the gaps were very wide, in this instance, I filled them in with a liberal amount of fiction. So here goes…

Bridget Lockwood had lived in Ecklington since she was born seventeen years ago. She worked the land with her parents. And the three of them lived happily in a small croft and survived through selling their produce to people in the village and surrounding towns. Every Tuesday on Market Day in the heart of Gloucester Bridget and her father would set up their cart in the town square to sell their home-grown vegetables. It was on one of those occasions that they encountered Mr Whittingham. Mr Whittingham was the head cook at Ecklington Manor House. He had travelled to Gloucester to look for a new supplier of vegetables for the Manor. Whittingham bought potatoes, sprouts and cabbages the first time. The next Tuesday he bought a greater variety of vegetables from the back of the cart. By the third week Mr Whittingham suggested that the Lockwoods would be paid well to deliver vegetables directly to Ecklington Manor each week. The extra journey was more than worth it for the Lockwood family as it doubled their weekly earnings.

After a few months, Bridget's father was introduced to the Lord of the Manor. Lord and Lady Ecklington, although privileged and from a very different social strata to Bridget's father, were kind and considerate to all of those who worked for them. They appreciated and acknowledged Mr Lockwood's service to the Manor and the quality of the produce. It wasn't long before Lockwood's vegetables, on Lord Eckington's recommendations, were also being sold at other neighbouring estates.

Within a couple of years, Bridget and her father were well known to all of the staff at Ecklington Manor. They would be welcomed into the kitchens by Mr Whittingham for a drink and a slice of cake, particularly if the weather had made the journey to the Manor difficult.

Three or four times a year Ecklington Manor would entertain local and not-so-local dignitaries. It so happened that one year, two days before Christmas, Lord and Lady Ecklington were to host a party. Over eighty guests would be wining and dining at the Manor House. Mr and Mrs Lockwood and their daughter, Bridget, were recruited to assist in the kitchens during the day and night and were assured that they could sleep in the servants' quarters at the end of the event.

At the end of the afternoon, having spent what seemed like days peeling potatoes, carrots and apples, Mr Whittingham asked Bridget if she would help out serving the food later on to the guests. An appropriate dress was found, a comb was run through her long dark hair and in no-time she was transformed into a servant.

Bridget was nervous at being involved at such a gathering. She had never set foot in any part of the Manor House apart from the kitchens, and she had never been in the same room as a Lord or Lady. She was reassured by Mr Whittingham that all she had to do was smile, be courteous and not drop any of the plates or dishes.

Bridget managed to smile, be courteous and not drop any plates or dishes. That is until the desserts were served. Apple tart was dished out in the kitchens and transported to the grand table by Bridget and the other servants.

Bridget was serving guests at one end of the long table where Lord Ecklington was sitting at the top of the table with his wife on one side and a youngish gentleman on the other side. As the young man was telling a story rather enthusiastically, one of his hands caught the dish that Bridget was trying to place in front of him. The apple tart ended up in his lap.

There was audible shock and gasps as the young man looked down at his trousers and then stared at Bridget who was looking as if the world was about to end. His stern look slowly turned to a smile.

"I've always found this to be the best place for a tart!" he proclaimed pointing at his lap.

The end of the table, including Lord and Lady Ecklington, started to laugh with the man. Bridget was too mortified to change her horrified expression, even if she understood his joke.

The man spoke again. This time directly at Bridget.

"Don't worry. It was an accident. If anything, it was my fault. I was waving my hands around like a mad man."

"I'm so sorry, Sir. No, it was my fault entirely. Let me get a cloth and wipe..."

"Thank you, that would be good, but I think I ought to do the wiping."

Bridget hurried off and returned in seconds with a cloth and another serving of apple tart.

"Here is the cloth, Sir, and another serving of dessert."

"That's very kind of you. What's your name?"

"My name is Bridget, Sir."

"Well Bridget, my name's John. I'm Lord and Lady Ecklington's son."

Lord Ecklington spoke up at this point. "You're Bridget Lockwood, aren't you? You and your parents supply us with our splendid vegetables, don't you?"

"Yes Sir. I was asked to help out with your party today, Sir. I'm so sorry."

"Bridget, it was an accident. Please don't worry about it. I'm sure my son has had hotter things than apple tart in his lap over the last year or so."

"Father, I don't know what you mean!"

Bridget smiled, because that's what she had been told to do and then politely exited the scene.

Later on, that night in the servants' quarters, Bridget was kept awake by the strangeness of not being in her own bed, the snoring of some others, including her mother in the next bunk, and the thoughts of John, the handsome son of the Lord of the Manor. Little did Bridget know that John was at the same time, in his own bed in a different part of the Manor house, thinking of the servant who dropped dessert in his lap. Her long dark hair, her hazel eyes, her shapely figure and her enchanting smile.

Bridget, her mother and father returned back home on Christmas Eve. They set a fire and celebrated Christmas with a glass of wine. The bottle of wine was a present from Lord Ecklington for helping out at the party.

In the new year, they returned to preparing the soil for the next growing cycle. Bridget and her father resumed their weekly journeys to Ecklington Manor to deliver food. She hoped that she would encounter Lord Ecklington's son on one of their visits, but it wasn't to be.

A year passed and the Lockwoods were recruited to help out at the Christmas party again. Bridget was on vegetable peeling duties again and yet again Mr Whittingham asked if she would help out upstairs like she did last year. She reluctantly agreed.

When the time came, a dress was brought to the kitchens. But this wasn't the dress that she wore last year. This was a very different looking dress. It was expensive. She was escorted by Mr Whittingham, not to the Great Hall but to a smaller room with just a small table and two chairs. The one chair was occupied by John Vaughan Ecklington and the other chair was for Bridget.

They dined together that night; the first night of many.

They fell in love across the table, across the divide.

They married two years later at Gloucester Cathedral.

Every Sunday morning they worshipped at church.

Every Sunday evening they ate apple tart.

They prayed to be blessed with a child.

God, sadly, did not answer their prayers.

But they thanked God for their fortune in finding each other.

John and Bridget spent many happy years together.

In later years, John prayed at Bridget's bedside when she became sick.

And John prayed one last time at her funeral that she would rise again.

And so, my story goes that John took his own life a few months' later. He was buried secretly in the grounds of Ecklington Manor by Mr Whittingham and some of the staff. In time he became a forgotten man.

But Bridget remains remembered.

Resurgamus.

AWAY FROM HOME

Please forgive me. This is not my first language. But I need to write my thoughts down.

I don't want these notes to sound as if I'm complaining. I'm not, I'm just angry and confused. But I am full of blame.

My name is Olena. I am now 31 years of age. I used to be a schoolteacher in a small village school, but not anymore. I spend my time now looking after my daughter on my own. My husband died about a year ago. I'm not sure of the exact date.

I remember sometime in late February 2022 when Russia declared war on our country (yet again), that my husband and I decided that we couldn't continue to stay in our village any longer. For several days and nights, we sat in our basement in our small house in Dzerkalne listening to gunfire and explosions. Our three-year-old daughter, Nataliya, cried herself to sleep, and so did we.

I wanted the three of us to leave the village we had made home. I was prepared to travel anywhere, anyhow to keep my family safe. I wanted my auntie, who also lived in Dzerkalne, to leave with us, but she refused. My husband also wanted to stay and fight back. He was insistent that he stayed and helped defend Ukraine against the Russian forces. He was a patriot who wanted to protect the country that he loved while knowing that his family was safe and well somewhere else, for the time being. He argued that Nataliya and I should leave our village immediately and find a temporary place to live in a safer part of Ukraine or in another country until the war was over. Once Ukraine had beaten back the Russian invasion and peace had been restored, then my daughter and I could return to our home and our old way of life.

My husband joined the resistance. My auntie, time and time again, refused to come with us. So, with a heavy heart we left our village with one suitcase of clothes between us and my mobile phone. I got on various trains with my daughter and travelled west across Ukraine and kept going through Europe until I reached England. Fortunately, I could read and speak some English so I could make myself understood to the people who were there organising us. I had to fill in a lot of forms and be interviewed by various people. These people found a hotel room for Nataliya and I to stay in while they looked for a family who would let us stay with them for some time, until we could return home. This was OK because there were other Ukrainian refugees staying in the same hotel. We would talk to each other about our experiences of the war and the terrible sights we had seen. We were so very grateful for the people in England who were giving us some temporary peace and shelter.

For a while I managed to text my husband and tell him that I was well and where we were. He would reply when he could and tell me that he was OK but he didn't go into too much detail about where he was positioned or what was happening. I understood that, but it didn't stop me worrying about him. But when the texts stopped arriving on my phone, I worried even more.

It was about three weeks' later that my worst fears were confirmed. My husband had been killed in action. A friend of a friend managed to contact me on my phone telling me that he'd been killed in a missile attack on a town about fifty miles away from where we lived. Apparently, my husband had been buried along with others in a temporary graveyard just a little way from the town.

So, there I was, a widow living in a hotel room with my daughter, who didn't understand war, death or why her mama was crying all of the time. My fellow Ukrainians in the hotel were supportive and kind, but one by one they were assigned families to stay with.

It must have been another two or three weeks before it was our turn to be 'homed' by a family. I was told that a couple had agreed to look after us for a while. They had two spare bedrooms in their house because both of their adult children had left home. They lived in a place called Sandy in Bedfordshire. I assumed it was a village by the sea. I was excited for Nataliya because I thought it would be her first chance to walk on a beach and play in an ocean. Unfortunately, that was not the case. Sandy was a quiet market town and seemed a long way from any ocean. I wasn't complaining though, as it felt like a million miles away from Russian bombs and bullets.

Tony and Sheila Williams were very welcoming and made Nataliya feel at home straight away. Apparently, once they knew that a young girl was staying with them, they went into their loft (that's what they call it in England) and brought down their own children's toys from when they were young and let my daughter play with them. They had been saving them for their own grandchildren but neither their son or daughter were looking to have children any time soon. We were also spoilt in other ways. Unlike the hotel, we had our own bedrooms and had a bathroom to ourselves as our hosts used their own en-suite. They trusted us to use the house as if it was our own, particularly during the day, when they both started work. Tony was the manager of a small factory in Sandy that made things, and Sheila worked all day in a small room downstairs in the house. She spent most of her time on the phone talking to people or tapping away at her computer.

Tony and Sheila were very generous and bought food that they thought we would both like. They let me have a key to the front door so that I could take Nataliya out during the day to get some fresh air and play in the local park. At night we would eat together and play games with Nataliya before bedtime. And when she was asleep, Tony would pour me a drink and they would let me talk about Ukraine, my life back home and my late husband. Sometimes Sheila would hug me on the settee when I started crying. Mr and Mrs Williams were great listeners and for a while became the parents I needed but hadn't had for a long time. I was so comfortable with them that I told them the bare bones of my life.

The youngest of three children. A reasonably happy childhood. But a difficult time as a teenager. At seventeen I left home one night and didn't return after yet another argument with my parents. I arrived at my Auntie's house in Dzerkalne one morning after travelling through the night to get there. My auntie contacted my parents that morning to tell them that I was safe. But that seemed to be it. They did not come for me. They did not ring me. So, I made a new life for myself in my auntie's village. My auntie encouraged me to continue my education. I went to college in Donetsk for three years and became a fully qualified teacher before returning to my auntie's small house where I started teaching in the local school.

One afternoon after school, I went for a walk, and got talking to a man who seemed to be working on a dilapidated house at the other end of the village. He had inherited the house from relatives, and he was planning to refurbish it before selling it.

Over the next three years, I helped him with the house and then we moved into it together, got married and had our daughter. We loved our daughter. We loved each other. We loved our life.

Then the bombing started. Ukrainians were injured and killed. Many of our houses were flattened. Our dreams were shattered.

It seemed that no-one from outside our country seemed to care at first. No-one helped us. All the other European countries would do is just help some of our citizens escape, but they wouldn't set foot inside our precious country to give assistance with the war. So, some of us left, while others stayed.

Some of us survived, while some of us died. I lived and my husband died.

When I described these events to Sheila and Tony I tried not to sound as if I was complaining. There were many people, many families from my home country in a much worse position than I was.

I showed them my sincere gratitude and tried, most of the time, to be optimistic about the future of my child and my country. After all, I was in a safe place called Sandy, living a normal life. But it wasn't normal. It wasn't real. It wasn't home.

I have no home now. My village was razed to the ground. I am certain that my auntie lost her life when the Russians occupied the village, but there is no way of knowing this for sure. So, I am left alone with my daughter in this foreign land. It is a friendly foreign country, but it is not home. Perhaps I don't know what home is anymore. I'm still running away, and I don't know where and when to stop.

I have lived with Tony and Sheila for over a year now and I promise you, I'm not complaining, but things have not always been easy. I am not blaming Mr and Mrs Williams. Not in the slightest. I was very fortunate to have hosts that were kind, sympathetic and comfortably well-off. I know some other Ukrainians have not been as lucky. Their hosts couldn't afford to keep funding the families that they were housing. After the UK government promised to cover the costs of Ukrainian refugees, it couldn't maintain it. In some houses I know that some hosts have decided not to continue with their offer to provide shelter. In other cases it has been cultural differences that have caused friction or unhappiness. Again, I have been fortunate as Tony and Sheila have been very accommodating. But I know this placement can't continue forever.

There have been a few tensions with their own children. I know that they and their partners would have liked to stay with their mother and father, but it is not very easy when we are using up two bedrooms. I have said that Nataliya and I could just use one bedroom, but Tony and Sheila insist that it is our home and we deserve to have our own rooms. This didn't go down well with their children, I think.

I have tried to ease the financial burden a little bit by getting a job. After six months I was accepted as a part-time Teaching Assistant at a local primary school and fortunately Nataliya was able to start Nursery at the same school. That gave Sheila back her house for at least some of the day and I contribute two thirds of my salary to the Williams to cover some of our costs. They were grateful and said that I didn't need to give them anything like that amount – but I insisted.

But no matter how lovely my hosts are, I still would prefer not to rely on them. And I'm sure, deep down, that although I try not to cause any difficulties for Tony and Sheila, that they would prefer not to have us living in their house. It was a unique and a generous act at first but after a while the novelty must have begun to wear off.

But what can I do? The war continues. There is no sign of a conclusion. And even if Russia retreated, where would I live? Where would most Ukrainians live who had homes on the east side of the country?

Would it be fair to take Nataliya back to the country that is in disarray? She is happy here in Sandy, England. Her English is better than mine now. She has some nice friends. More than me, really.

There are a few teachers and TAs at my school who have been friendly, and we have gone to a few of their houses at weekends for playdates with their children. It has been lovely to see Nataliya being happy with children of her own age. It's amazing how quickly she has adjusted to her new way of life. She has almost forgotten her time in Ukraine. I wish I could.

One of the TAs heard me crying in the staff toilets one day. Donna thought I had had a difficult time in the classroom, but I explained that I missed my home country, I missed being a teacher and having a loving partner.

Donna took it upon herself to find me a 'friend' on a dating site. I wasn't used to doing this. It also felt as if I was betraying my dead husband but after a while, I said I would try it.

My hosts approved of me trying to re-invent myself. Perhaps they were hoping that I would find a man to marry and then I would no longer need to live with them. Perhaps I was wrong. That sounds mean. And I don't want to be mean about Tony and Sheila. They don't deserve it. They did warn me about some of the men that might be out there on these dating sites, so I was careful in writing my profile. I explained that

I was Ukrainian and a single mother. I explained that I was a teaching assistant and I lived with a lovely couple who took me in when I moved to Sandy. I didn't want there to be any misunderstandings. I tried to make it clear what I didn't want from a man as well. I didn't want someone to 'look after me' because I was a poor refugee. I didn't want an instant father-figure for Nataliya. But I also didn't want a man who thought that buying me a drink or a meal would somehow lead to some sort of immediate payback. So, my friend from school helped me choose a few men that might be OK as friends, maybe.

I started texting them and they texted me back but after a few weeks only one man seemed to be serious about our friendship. We then spoke on our phones for a while before we decided to meet up in Sandy for a meal at a local restaurant.

Sheila was very kind and helped me choose a pretty dress from a local clothes shop in Sandy. "That's perfect - pretty, but not too sexy for a first date" she commented and promptly paid for it. She is so kind.

Donna also helped me. Once she knew the time and the place, I was meeting Frank, she persuaded her partner to take her out to the same restaurant so that she could keep an eye on me, or more importantly, my date.

Although Sheila and Donna were just wanting me to be safe and happy, I felt as if they were treating me as if I was fourteen. I did not need to be protected. I had been through a lot in my life already. I was a survivor, so I could cope with a bad date.

As it turned out, it wasn't a bad date. It was nice. Nice enough for a second date a few days later, without Donna needing to be there. This time we went to a pub in Sandy for a couple of drinks. Fortunately, this meant that I could wear my jeans as I didn't possess another dress, pretty or otherwise. After a lovely evening, Frank walked me home. He seemed very nice.

The next time we met was on a Saturday afternoon in our local park. Frank wanted to meet Nataliya without it being too formal. The three of us then went to McDonalds for tea and Frank paid. It may have been the Happy Meal or the ice cream he got for her in the park, but from then on he was a big hit with my daughter.

I was still a little bit reluctant to consider my relationship with Frank as anything other than a friendship. I realised that I couldn't look too far ahead or become optimistic about the future. What had happened in Ukraine prevented me from looking forward. I still spent most of my time looking back.

But as the weeks passed, I saw Frank twice a week. He took me and Nataliya to see his parents in his hometown of Bedford followed by a takeaway meal at his flat close to where his parents lived. Frank had been through a difficult divorce just before the pandemic struck the UK. He was presently doing two part-time jobs to pay his way. Some nights he worked in a care home for the elderly and then some days he drove a delivery van. It meant that we had to organise our times to see each other very carefully, but we managed.

Sheila and Tony invited Frank over for a meal one Sunday lunch time. It was a lovely occasion. The five of us around a table eating a roast dinner. Just for an hour or two I felt like I was part of a bigger family. I almost felt as if I was home.

But then when I went to bed that night, I thought about all my fellow Ukrainians, not the ones dispersed around the world but the ones who stayed to fight for our country. What would they think of me now? While they are living in bombed-out squalor, fearing that each day may be their last, eating scraps and hiding away – there I was today, having a roast dinner with foreigners making me feel like I'm at home.

Well, I'm not. I have fled my country to live a safe life while my country and my people burn. What will history make of the likes of me? What will Nataliya think of me in years to come? Will she think that I was heroic and made a huge sacrifice to keep her alive or will she think I was a coward to abandon my homeland?

What do I do?

Do I stay in England? Do I remain here so that Nataliya can become an English citizen? If she stays here the chances are that she will have a good education and a successful life. Do I settle down with Frank? Will Frank and I marry and have children? English children. Will I forget where I came from?

Do I go back to Ukraine? Do I go back now and help the war effort? Do I wait until the war is over? What would I say to those who stayed and survived? Should I find my husband's grave and afford him a decent burial? Would it be fair to Nataliya to take her back to her birth country? Would Frank come with me?

I don't know. It would be unfair on my daughter to take her back to Ukraine. And I can't expect Frank to give up his life in England for me.

Perhaps I should go back on my own. Leave Nataliya here in Sandy. She would be looked after; I know she would. There are Sheila and Tony, Donna and her boyfriend, Frank and his parents. She would have a good life in England. But I don't deserve that life. I deserted my country. The country that needed me. I left my husband. He needed me. I must make amends. I may hate Putin but I hate myself more. I need to do this. But when?

The people in England have generally been so kind and understanding to us, but sooner or later we will be treated like all the other immigrants in England. Their sympathies will fade, and we will be regarded differently. Refugees turned to immigrants. Wanted to unwanted.

I should go home…soon.

But when will I be able to decide?

Only God and Putin know.

But one thing is certain, as I write my thoughts down, I think I'll feel homeless wherever I live, today and tomorrow.

TO HAVE AND NOT HAVE

Part One

I was excited. My first serious holiday. I hadn't been away properly for a long time. I'd stayed with friends for a couple of nights here and there. But nothing extravagant. I couldn't afford anything luxurious. And I couldn't afford to leave my job for a week let alone two weeks. Not until now.

I hadn't won the lottery, if that's what you're thinking. Well, I suppose I did in a way, a while back. I met a man. A good-looking, kind and considerate man who had a very good job and wanted me, even though I was not the most desirable catch on the planet. I wasn't wealthy, I wasn't pin-up material and I had some past and present baggage (and I'm not talking about holiday luggage!) But he still wanted me and I wanted him…even though I was married.

Oh yes, I forgot to tell you that bit of my story… or did I try to avoid telling you that? OK. You can start to judge me if you like. I can hear you calling me all sorts of names. Go ahead! I suppose I deserve it. Here I am about to fly to the Caribbean for a two-week holiday with a fabulous man and I am, in the eyes of the law, still married to someone else. I'd been seeing this man without my husband's knowledge for some time, before I admitted it. Notice I didn't say ex-husband. We are still married although I don't want to be. But that's another story or in this case another part of the same story.

I married my husband in our early twenties after 'going steady' for a few years. He joined the army as soon as he could after school and I worked in a shop. I suppose I fell in love with this hunk and hulk of a uniformed man. He was a gentle giant and I was the little woman that he wanted to protect. We loved each other, we had a home on the barracks and our plan was to have at least two children. That was the plan, but the army had other ideas. They deployed him wherever and whenever they wanted to. I hardly ever saw him. But I did have the company of other wives and girlfriends who lived on the base.

I worried about my husband most of the time. Where was he? Was he safe? When would I see him again? And, to be fair, he worried about me. He felt guilty for leaving me all alone for months and months at a time. These long absences from each other were not good for either of us. It was slowly changing both of us and our relationship. Not much of a married life.

After serving ten years in the army he decided, with my blessing, that it was time for him to quit. We would find a normal place to live, he would get a normal job and we would try to lead a normal life on civvy street and rekindle our marriage.

We rented a place in the local town, close to the barracks, so that we still had some connections with friends on the base. My husband started looking for jobs. He had very few qualifications to brag about, but he did have ten years' service in the armed forces in his favour. Unfortunately, most jobs he looked at wanted exam certificates. After a couple of months and through necessity he got a job as a doorman at a nightclub in town. A doorman is a slightly fancier title than a bouncer, but the job description was basically the same. He worked 5 sessions a week – from 7.00 at night until 2.00 in the morning, but he was rarely home until 3.00am. He didn't enjoy the job, but it paid slightly more than the minimum wage. With my wages at the shop, we could just about cover the rent and save a little towards a deposit on a small, terraced house. In a couple of years' time we could start the family that we both wanted.

This arrangement was not perfect by any means. I worked six days a week at the shop. And most days when I got back to the flat we shared a meal before he left for the nightclub leaving me alone most evenings.

Once a week I went out for a drink with some of the women who I knew from the barracks. They were a good laugh and were often happy to get drunk and flirt with guys while their partners were serving our country overseas. They were a good and a bad influence on me. They would sometimes end up going on to the town's night club after drinking far too much. I would always decline the offer. I didn't want to drink and dance at a club where I knew my husband worked on the door. It would have been weird.

On one such night at about 10.00pm, having drank far too much at the pub, my friends suggested going to the nightclub for an hour or so. I told them to go ahead as I was too tired and tipsy and would walk home. It was only five minutes in the opposite direction.

When they left, I put on my coat and picked up my handbag and walked steadily to the door. When the cold night air hit me, my body reacted, and I began to feel dizzy.

"Are you alright?" I heard a voice ask me.

"Sorry, were you talking to me?" I replied to the man standing vaping outside the front of the pub.

"Yes, don't take this the wrong way but you look a bit worse for wear."

"Well thank you very much!"

"I didn't mean how you're dressed or look…I meant that you are acting as if you've had one more drink than you are used to…in fact you look great, by the way…sorry…I'll stop talking now…I sound like I'm hitting on you or a pervert or something…sorry…I've really got to stop opening my mouth…I was just worried about how you're going to get home."

I don't know why but after another five or ten minutes more banter, I let him walk me home. Then a few nights later I let him take me for a drink. Two more dates later I let him kiss me. Then a few nights after that I started sleeping with him.

I would go to his three-bedroomed house after my husband left for work in the evening and he would drop me back at the flat by 2.00 am at the latest where I pretended to be asleep by the time my husband got back from the nightclub.

I felt really happy, for the first time in years but I also felt incredibly guilty about being unfaithful. And I knew in my heart of hearts that I couldn't carry on like this. Something had to change.

Within a few months my new man wanted me to leave my husband, move in with him and start a new life with him. He had a great job, a great house and he didn't need me to work in the shop. He said that I deserved better than the life I was tolerating at the moment.

After seven months of deceit, I had made up my mind. I could not lie to myself or my husband anymore. At the next opportunity I sat my husband down and told him what had been going on and that I loved someone else and was moving in with him. My big strong husband cried like a baby. He begged me to stay and said that he would try to make everything better. I asked him how he could do that, but he wasn't able to change my mind.

I told him that I would not ask for a divorce yet but that there should be a trial separation for six months before we discussed our marriage again.

I moved out and moved in with my new man the next night while my husband was at work.

I cut off contact with him during those next six months. I didn't go for a drink with my girlfriends from the army base. I began to enjoy my new life and put my old life behind me.

When my new partner talked about marriage, I knew I had to talk to my husband. I tried his mobile, but the number was discontinued. I went to the flat to talk to him but there were new tenants in the flat. I went to the nightclub but discovered he didn't work there anymore.

I can still divorce him, but it won't be by mutual consent. It's more likely that my solicitor will claim that my husband deserted me.

I just want this sorted out. I hope my husband is happy and that he has found someone else. Or perhaps he's re-joined the army? Anyway, it's not my concern anymore.

I'm about to go on a romantic holiday. A lovely hotel room with a balcony overlooking the sea. I'm packing a couple of sexy bikinis and some lacey underwear. We've decided that I should come off the pill and start the family we both want. Life is getting better.

Part Two

The hardest thing about my life at the moment is trying to appear to be normal. To pretend to be just like everyone else. A steady job. A roof over my head. A loving family.

And yet every morning I wake up cold and hungry and wanting to leave the place I have stayed overnight, knowing full well that I will return there within a week.

Yes, I have a job. Cash in hand, less than minimum wage but it's a job. It pays for food, a few hot drinks and petrol for the car. These are the things I need more than anything else. I would like more but I can't afford it.

I can't afford rent and the council will not supply me with a place to live because I am still married, if in name only. They told me to go and live with my wife but how can I? She's living with a rich guy in his house. I don't think they would appreciate me living with them.

So I live in my small van. The van that I drive around in during the day and sleep in at night. I work for a guy with a window cleaning business. Every two-storey house I clean costs £14. For every house I clean I get £4. The rest goes to my boss. I have to keep records of each house I clean. And every night I have to show him my records and divide up the takings. I'm lucky if I make £60 in a day and then I have to pay for my own petrol travelling around the towns and surrounding areas.

Half of the van is taken up with window cleaning equipment and the other half is my travelling house and home. Luckily, with my years in the army, I am used to living in difficult conditions but it's not easy day after day, and particularly, night after night.

I have had to cope with a great deal in the last six months or so since I was booted out of the flat that I had shared with my wife. I couldn't pay the rent on my own, so I had to leave. I also lost my job as doorman at a nightclub when I literally lost it with a guy as he was waiting to enter the club and told me with a smirk on his face, that he had seen my wife cosying-up to another guy in a fancy restaurant. I wiped the smirk off his face and lost my job there and then.

Since then, I have learnt to control my temper and I am beginning to take control of my life, however limited it is. I was sofa-surfing at a few mates' houses before my welcome wore thin. I slept on the street for a while and then I managed to get this job working for this guy as a window cleaner. I don't know if he realises that I use his van as my home, but he doesn't seem to care as long as I hand him his money at the end of each day.

I can't get a proper job because I don't have a permanent home address. But I can't earn and save enough money to even get a deposit for a flat. Even if I could, the rents are far too high on the sorts of cash-in-hand work I can get. So, I'm stuck at the bottom of a deep muddy bunker without any way of climbing out.

You need to know a lot in order to survive when you're living and sleeping on the open road. You have to be organised and prepared. Better organised and prepared than when I was in a war zone.

I have various different sized zip-up bags for different things – toiletries, clothes, utensils, bedding and personal belongings. Then, of course, there's a bucket.

I have a couple of small sheets to hang as curtains at night over the two windows at the back of the van for privacy. I have to leave one of the front windows slightly open to let some air in and out even on cold nights.

I use 24-hour service stations on local motorways as much as possible. I alternate between three different service stations at night. I put in a couple of gallons of petrol at a time. If I get a cheap breakfast and meal in the evening from these places, it means that I can use their washing facilities in the morning and at night.

I spend a couple of evenings a week in laundrettes to keep warm. And on the other nights I treat myself to one long drink at a pub to stay out of the cold for as long as possible. Those few hours in the pub help me feel normal.

On a Sunday I go to church for an hour for something to do. And I walk around the markets looking for bargains.

Just living in a vehicle is really difficult. It feels as if it is illegal and yet people do because they have nowhere else to live. Very few places will allow you to park overnight so you have to be inventive. This is what I do:

I try to find places without CCTV to park up.

I only use car parks that are not gated at night.

I don't use the same place twice in one week.

If I park roadside outside houses, then I wait till all the lights are off and people have gone to bed. Then I try to leave before they get up in the morning and notice the van.

I try to keep on the move as much as I can and then I won't be reported to the police.

I make sure that all of my doors are locked from the inside.

I stay as quiet as possible as I don't want to attract any attention.

I try to be anonymous. Nondescript. A nobody in this beloved country.

And yet I fought for this country. I risked my life overseas for this country. But no-one cares now. Not the government, not my wife.

Will my life get any better?

THE HOT AND COLD CAFÉ

No Marmite

Come rain or shine Mr Raymond Brownlee walked each morning along the high street to buy his newspaper from Mr Singh's newsagents.

"Good morning, Mr Singh."

"Good morning, Mr Brownlee. It's cats and dogs out there. Good job you brought your umbrella."

"Indeed."

"Here's your paper. Are you sure you don't want us to deliver it to you each day? We can have it posted through your letter box by 8.30 in the morning…even on a Sunday."

"No, it's fine. It does me good to have a bit of exercise each morning," replied Brownlee paying his daily 70 pence. "I'll see you tomorrow."

"OK. Remember it's Saturday tomorrow. Your paper is twice the price at weekends."

Raymond Brownlee stepped outside the newsagents, flipped open his umbrella and tucked his newspaper under his coat. He walked 150 yards down the high street and turned into the Hot N' Cold Café.

"Morning Mr B," said Sheila Nicholls, the owner of the cafe, from behind the counter. "Usual?"

"Yes please," replied Brownlee as he headed for a small table by the front window of the cafe. On the way to his table, he hung up his overcoat and umbrella on a coat peg and settled down at the table with his paper. He briefly surveyed his surroundings and noticed a few regulars sitting at different tables. He nodded to some of them and mouthed good morning to an elderly lady who was tucking into a hot drink and a slice of chocolate cake. She was a frequent visitor to the café at this time each day.

Raymond could not imagine eating cake at this time in the morning. He was having his usual savoury breakfast of two rounds of white toast with Marmite and a pot of tea.

Within a couple of minutes his breakfast arrived at his table delivered by Sheila.

"There we are Mr. B."

"Thank you."

"It's a wet one today, isn't it?"

"Indeed."

And with that Sheila returned to her position behind the counter.

For the next hour or so Mr Brownlee shut out the hustle and bustle of the cafe and slowly consumed his tea and toast. He read various pages of the newspaper before attempting the crossword. He also stared at the pedestrians outside - a mixture of commuters walking towards bus stops or the train station, and shoppers heading towards necessities or bargains. He liked to people-watch from a distance. He was not a great talker these days, but he did like to look at his fellow human beings who lived in his town, albeit through a glass barrier.

Raymond felt that this was his town as he was born, raised, schooled, and he worked here all of his life. Other than holidays, he had never left. He hadn't gone to university and when he left school at 16, he'd started working at the local bank and remained there until he retired some five years ago.

Although he had lived in the town for almost seventy years, he was far from being a well-known personality. He was a quiet child at school and then a quiet single man, and then a quiet married man. He met Florence when he was into his thirties. Florence and Raymond led a quiet, contented life for just over thirty years until she fell ill and succumbed to bowel cancer. Since the funeral and his retirement, Raymond had lived a solitary life, only venturing out of the house for food and cash. He no longer wanted to go on holidays. There were no family members to visit, so he stayed inside his house most of the time.

"What did you eat?" said a small voice in earshot of Brownlee.

Raymond continued to work out nine down on the cryptic crossword.

"What did you eat, Mister?" said the voice again.

Raymond looked around this time to see a young boy sitting by himself at an adjacent table.

"Oh hello. Were you talking to me?" asked Raymond.

"Granny is getting me a cake. She's over there. What did you eat?"

"Well, I had some toast with Marmite on it. It was good."

"I like Marmite, but Granny doesn't. She likes jam."

"Are you looking forward to your cake?"

"Yes. I chose it at the counter and then Granny told me to sit down while she paid for it."

"I see."

"Granny looks after me sometimes because mommy has to work."

"I expect you have a nice time at your Granny's house, don't you?"

"Yes. I love going to Granny's. This is her. With my cake."

"Well, well, well. I see you've been making friends while I was at the counter," said the boy's grandmother as she sat down.

"Where's my cake, Granny?"

"The lady behind the counter will bring our drinks and food over in a minute, sweetheart."

"This man had toast with Marmite."

"Did he now? I hope you didn't bother him, James? He was quietly reading the newspaper and then you came along and disturbed him."

Raymond looked round and smiled at James' grandmother. "It's fine. I was struggling with the crossword, so it was a welcome distraction."

"That's nice of you to say but James can be a little…forward…when it comes to talking to people. He's going to keep his teachers on their toes when he starts school in September," the grandmother said, smiling at her grandson and at Raymond.

"I'm sure his teachers will enjoy his company…I did. I don't talk to many people these days…big or small."

"Are you retired then?"

"Yes. I used to work in the bank along the high street until a few years ago."

"I thought I recognised you. We used to bank there…I mean…I still do. Weren't you the manager there?"

"I was. For the last eighteen years of my career. I finished just after my wife, Florence, passed away and just before the pandemic started. I don't go out much now. I collect the newspaper every day and read it in here while I have my breakfast. That seems to be my routine these days. What about you?"

"Since my divorce ten years ago I've been filling up my time with my two daughters' families. Baby-sitting, childcare and school runs. I've joined a few clubs and societies at the local U3A. I'm also trying to learn to play bridge…"

"Granny…I've finished my cake and pop."

"Good boy James. Well done. I suppose we ought to get going then. It's been nice talking to you…erm…"

"Raymond Brownlee…but please call me Ray…it's about time somebody else did…other than my wife."

"Well, Ray, thank you for the company. I'm sure James and I will see you again. Goodbye for now."

"Bye-bye," said James waving at Raymond as he left the Hot N' Cold Café with his grandmother.

***

"Good morning, Mr Singh."

"Good morning, Mr Brownlee. Here's your paper. A nice spring morning. Summer will soon be here."

"Indeed," replied Brownlee, paying his 70 pence. "I'll see you tomorrow."

At the Hot N' Cold Café Raymond laid out his newspaper on his usual table and waited for his breakfast to arrive.

Raymond was a few minutes into the crossword when James and his grandmother entered the café.

"Granny, there's Mr Brownlee, can I go and talk to him while you order the food."

"Well…just while I get our food, if he doesn't mind."

"Hello Mr Brownlee," said James as he walked over to Brownlee's table.

"Well…hello there James, do you want to sit down?"

"Thanks."

"Is your granny getting you a cake?"

"Yes…and some orange squash. Mommy says I can only have pop at the weekends."

"Well, it's Friday today, so you'll be able to have some pop tomorrow."

69

"Hello Mr Brownlee. Nice to see you again."

"And you. Please call me Ray. Both of you. Why don't I pull up another chair and then you can join James and me?"

"Well…if you're sure we're not bothering you."

"Not at all," said Raymond as he stood up and moved another chair over to the table. "Please sit…erm…"

"Oh…I'm sorry…my name's Gwen. Gwen Forbes. Or Granny or Granny Gwen to some…but please, Ray, just call me Gwen," said Gwen smiling at James and Ray.

"Mr Ray, can I ask you something?" asked James.

"What would you like to know?" replied Ray.

"Why do you read a newspaper in the café?"

"Well, I like to know what's going on in the world."

"But why don't you just use the internet or watch the news on TV?"

"James! Not everyone is like your mom and dad. I'm afraid, James's parents are never off their phones, tablets and laptops. They live by their gadgets. I'm afraid I'm old school."

"Nothing wrong with that. I'm as old school as you…not that I think you're old, Gwen…"

"Why, thank you kind sir, but my body is beginning to tell me otherwise."

"Aches and pains?"

"A few aches in my joints every so often. And my grandkids are the pains…" said Gwen, nudging James and smiling at him.

"Granny! I'm not a pain…am I?"

"No…not really…well…not all of the time…"

"Just during the waking hours," said Ray, winking at Gwen.

"Granny, I've finished my cake."

"Well, I suppose we ought to let Ray have some peace and quiet then. Put your coat on and say goodbye to Ray."

"Bye-bye Mr Ray. See you again."

"Bye Ray. Thanks for the company."

"Any time. I'm here most days. Bye."

"Morning, Mr Singh."

"Good morning, Mr Brownlee. Chilly today. Winter will soon be here."

"Indeed," replied Brownlee. "Can I have a copy of The Beano and a block of Dairy Milk, please."

"No newspaper?"

"No Thanks. Bye."

At The Hot N' Cold Café Ray could see through the window that Gwen was already sitting at their table.

"Morning Mr B. Gwen's already ordered. I'll bring it over in a minute," said Sheila from behind the counter.

"Thank you, Sheila."

Ray moved to their table. Gwen smiled.

"Hello."

"Hello."

"I've just dropped James off at school. His first day at school. It was quite emotional."

"Don't worry, he'll quickly make friends and he'll charm his teacher by the end of the day. I bought him a comic and a chocolate bar for being a brave lad. Will you give it to him later?"

"Of course. That's really nice of you."

"It's not a problem. In fact, selfishly, it's rather nice of James to give the two of us some time together."

"You realise that you won't be able to read your newspaper if you're sitting with me."

"I've stopped buying it now. I'm hoping that we could make this a part of our new routine each day."

"I would like that very much. I've also booked you in for beginners' bridge for tomorrow afternoon. I told the instructor that you will be my partner."

"That sounds perfect."

Sheila brought a tray of food over to the table.

"Here we are. A pot of tea for two and four rounds of white toast with jam. No Marmite," Sheila smiled, "enjoy!"

"We will indeed," they replied and gently touched hands.

Marmite

Linda sat wondering what the hell she was doing here. But it was Linda's own fault. She'd decided on the place, the date and the time. She couldn't blame anyone else...only herself...for being in this position.

Linda sat there, on her own, wondering about the next hour or so and, ultimately, the next year or so. Linda tried to look occupied rather than pre-occupied by staring at her phone reading old Twitter messages, texts and emails and scrolling down her Facebook pages. She punctuated this mindless activity with looking up and surveying the scene.

The table she chose was at the back of the Hot N' Cold Café, which meant that she had an easy view of customers entering. The café was half full but had a pleasant, relaxed atmosphere to it. Not that Linda was feeling relaxed, but that was her problem, not the café's. In fact, the lady who served her at the counter and brought her coffee over to her was lovely. She made a point of chatting to Linda and making her feel welcome and at home in the café. Not that this was home for Linda. She was a good half-an-hours' drive from her house which meant a lot of petrol for a cup of coffee. But, of course, a coffee wasn't the reason she drove all this way. And she certainly wasn't going to tell the woman at the counter her real reason. That was her business and no-one else's.

Linda was fascinated by the couple sitting at the front of the café. They were both in their sixties and enjoying each other's company. They were clearly in love. Linda wondered how long they had been married. Probably thirty years or more and they were still discreetly touching hands and staring into each other's eyes. Linda remembered those times and those feelings as if they were yesterday - but sadly they were yesterday, many yesterdays' ago. Linda was twenty years or so younger than the couple at the window, but she was envious of them. Their love was not stale.

While Linda waited, she reflected on her own life and loves. Her family. Her mother gave birth to her 43 years ago. Her parents' second child. Her older sister, Helen, was now 47. Their mom and dad were teachers and they lived in a modest detached house on the outskirts of

Bromsgrove. Looking back, Linda felt that the first twenty years of her life were reasonably happy. She loved her parents and her older sister. She did well at school, specialised in the Humanities at A level and went to Keele University to study European History. When Linda's sister, Helen, graduated from Birmingham University she did not return to her parents' house, but she and her boyfriend decided to travel abroad and enjoy a gap year before starting work and having their own family. As it transpired, they did not return to England. They set up camp in New Zealand and never looked back. Linda somehow felt betrayed and shunned by her older sister and over time they lost close contact and that invisible bond that bound them together loosened its grip.

After Linda graduated, she returned home with a 2:1 degree and no idea what she wanted to do for a career. And things were not the same at home. Her sister was gone and her parents felt like strangers to her. They also seemed like strangers to each other. In the next few years Linda had a series of unsuccessful relationships and jobs in offices. Her life at home also became less and less comfortable to the point that she made the decision to rent a flat on the other side of Bromsgrove. Linda would pop back to see her parents once a week and on one occasion they announced that they were separating and selling the house. In the next few visits Linda discovered that her mother and father had been "estranged" for some time and had found other partners. Linda felt betrayed again and her separate visits to her separated parents with their new live-in lovers became less frequent.

Linda's family had dissolved in front of her eyes in a matter of a few years since she had left university. She was living in a rented flat, paid for by a job she didn't like that much. The only good thing about her life was that she had found a nice guy at work who was attracted to her. Mark was her line manager at her office. They had gradually realised that their professional relationship was blurring into a personal relationship. Within a year, they were engaged and within another eighteen months, they were married. Her parents and new partners came to the wedding and Helen made the trip from New Zealand to see her sister get hitched. Although it was great that the family was back together for a short time, it also emphasised to all of them that they had all moved on and away from each other.

That was some fifteen years ago, and they had not all been in the same room at the same time since then. But over the years her old family was replaced by her new family...Mark. He was a solid guy, reliable and caring. She could now make plans to extend her new family with children.

After a lot of baby-making activity over the next ten years, Linda and Mark reluctantly accepted that there were not going to be any little additions to the family...it was just going to be the two of them.

As time went on their acceptance turned to silent resentment and indifference towards each other. And this is how it had been for several years now.

Linda stared at her empty coffee cup. She felt alone. Living in a loveless marriage with a family that felt like they were a million miles away from her heart and home.

Linda's close friends were worried about her and advised her to re-invent herself. She should not settle for this life as she moved into middle age. They wanted her to do something different. Join a gym. Change her job. Move to New Zealand to be near her sister or get a divorce. But Linda wasn't keen to change.

As the months passed Linda became more and more dissatisfied with her partner and her life generally and so she decided it was time for a change before it was too late.

So here she was in this café. Staring at an empty cup. Waiting for a change of heart.

She had found the very thought of a dating site repugnant. A married woman of her age going on a site felt not just weird but embarrassing and desperate. Particularly as she was doing this behind Mark's back.

After secretly signing up and paying for a six-month period on the site, Linda had created a profile of herself that was not too far from the truth but was not too near the truth, either. Not that Mark could probably care less if she intended to find someone new. He was probably finding solace elsewhere. He spent several evenings in the week drinking with his mates and having time away from the office attending conferences or training courses. But Linda still found this subterfuge disconcerting.

Each night Linda and Mark would lie next to each other in bed without any contact and each day they would work in the same set of offices on the same floor of their workplace, as if nothing was wrong. But they knew that the professional distance they had at work was now a personal distance at home.

Linda looked at her watch. Five minutes to go.

After three months' swiping left and right on her phone while sitting on the loo at home, she had found someone who understood her situation and seemed nice and looked attractive. After another month of texts between them they had decided to meet up. Somewhere neutral. Somewhere safe.

Linda didn't know how this would progress. The most likely scenario would be that the meeting was a complete disaster. Or it may be OK but there was no spark between them. Or it might be just a quick kiss and fumble in one of their cars before never seeing each other again. Or maybe, just maybe, they would fall in love, Linda would get a quickie divorce and they would be married within a year.

Two minutes to go.

Linda had got to the café far too early. Was this a sign of how desperate she was?

She looked up to see the nice old couple who were sitting by the window getting up from their seats. The man helped his partner on with her coat and left his arm on her shoulder to steer her to the door. What a gentleman. What a lovely couple.

One minute to go.

Linda decided that if her date had not arrived in the next eleven minutes, she would go. She had told Mark that she was having a day off using her annual leave to visit an old 'friend' who she hadn't seen for ages. Well, that was partly true, other than it was a new 'friend' who she had never met before!

Linda foraged about in her handbag on the floor for her make-up mirror and quickly gave her face and hair the once-over. She hoped she wouldn't be a disappointment.

She bent down and slipped her mirror back in her bag.

"Lydia?"

Linda looked up and then sat up straight.

"I'm a few seconds late as I didn't want to appear to0 eager, but I couldn't wait any longer. I was pacing up and down the high street for the last ten minutes."

"I must admit, I got here early and found a quiet table at the back of the café. I hope this is OK?"

"Lydia, this is perfect."

"I suppose, if we mean to get off on the right track I ought to be totally honest with you. My real name is not Lydia, it's Linda."

"Well in that case, my real name is not Joy, it's Joyce."

They smiled at each other across the table and shook hands in a relaxed and trusting way. Their hands gently touching each other's while they enjoyed two coffees and two servings of Marmite on toast.

Jam Today

"Good morning, Mr Singh."

"Good morning, Mr Brownlee. Newspaper?"

"No, thank you, not today, just this box of chocolates, please."

"Certainly. That will be £8.99."

"Here's a ten-pound note."

"Thank you. It's good to see some people still use cash. Here's your change, Mr Brownlee."

"Thank you, Mr Singh. I will see you soon."

Mr Brownlee walked out of the shop, uncharacteristically whistling, and headed along the high street for the Hot N' Cold Café.

"Good morning, Mr Brownlee," said Sheila Nicholls from behind the counter, as he entered the empty café, "Are you going to order now, or do you want to wait until your…friend arrives?"

"I'll wait, if that's OK?" he replied and walked towards his usual table.

"That's fine," said Sheila. Sheila's phone pinged and she glanced down at the text and smiled to herself.

"Actually," announced Sheila, putting on her coat, "I've just got to pop out of the café for five minutes to get some supplies. If anyone comes in, would you mind telling them I will be back very soon."

"I will hold the fort," said Raymond, smiling at Sheila.

Sheila scurried along the high street to the newsagents. Mr Singh, who was serving an elderly customer, acknowledged Sheila as she walked in, nodded and smiled. Sheila looked along the shelves for some items for the café. Mr Singh helped the customer, with her bag of supplies, to the front door. He opened the door and waved her off down the road, then closed and locked the front door and flicked the sign on the door over from 'Open' to 'Be Back Soon'.

Mr Singh walked over to Sheila.

"Can I help you?"

"Well, I'm hoping that you can. I can't find what I'm looking for in the front of the shop. I was wondering if you have it in the storeroom in the back?"

Mr Singh took hold of Sheila's hand and led her past the counter into the storeroom. "I think I've got just what you're looking for, if you wouldn't mind coming with me."

"My pleasure," said a smiling Sheila.

***

Sheila returned to her café twenty minutes later carrying a jar of strawberry jam that she grabbed on the way out of the newsagents.

"Sorry, so sorry," said Sheila to the people who were sitting in the café waiting for their drinks and food. "I needed some jam, and it took me a while to get it…"

Gwen smiled sympathetically at Sheila as she placed the jar on the counter and took her coat off. "It's not a problem, Sheila. Take a moment. You look a bit flustered," said Gwen.

"Yes, I'm a bit out of breath," said Sheila and announced to the customers that the first round of drinks were free of charge as she'd kept them all waiting.

Ten minutes later Sheila's heart rate had normalised, and it was back to business as usual. She'd first served a pot of tea and four rounds of toast with strawberry jam to Gwen and Mr Brownlee. Then she made a coffee and an orange squash for a mother and her toddler. Finally, Sheila served the two women at the back of the café who were now regulars and becoming very close 'friends'.

Sheila contemplated the term 'business as usual.' How usual was it for a middle-aged woman to have a series of 'business meetings' at the back of the newsagents or in the storeroom of a café? And this series of discreet meetings had been going on for a while now. This secret relationship was not borne out of cheating on other parties as neither of them were involved in other partnerships. They were not hurting anyone else. They were both single and had been for some time. They were both in their forties and had their own bank accounts. It was a free country. So why not go public? And why did it feel wrong to be so private? Was it the excitement of the affair? Although it wasn't really an affair. They were happy in this arrangement and no-one else would be unhappy if they found out. They both enjoyed their short times of closeness together and they also both enjoyed their times apart. No 24/7 commitments. Just two friends bonding from time to time, when the mood or urge took them.

Sheila remembered their very first meeting over four months ago. She was on her way to the café one May morning when her mind was consumed by winning the Roll-Over Lottery in that night's draw. £57 million. That would do very nicely. She could pay off her debts, buy a mansion in London outright, have a fleet of fancy cars and a yacht, go on a world cruise and still have enough money left over to buy another lottery ticket. There was only one problem…she didn't buy lottery tickets! Not until today. She would get one at the local newsagents. So Sheila walked into Mr Singh's newsagents with the intention of having a life-changing experience.

"Morning," said Sheila.

"Good morning. A nice day isn't it. The forecast says bright and sunny all day," replied the man behind the counter.

"Let's hope so. Good weather can be good for business."

"Oh, does your business rely on good weather then?"

"No, not directly. I run the café up the road. But if the weather is nice then more people shop on the high street and then more shoppers come into the café."

"I understand. Whereas most of my customers are regulars, come rain or shine."

"Anyway, I've just popped in for a lottery ticket. It's a roll-over apparently. It just could be my lucky day."

"I hope so."

Sheila used her lucky numbers and paid for the ticket.

"I should be a multi-millionaire by tomorrow," Sheila said, kissing the ticket.

"Either way, I hope you'll become a regular."

"If I win, I think I'll be on a cruise ship by the weekend."

"Well, I hope you remember who supplied you the ticket."

"I will…Mr…?"

"Singh, Sandeep Singh, but most people call me Sandy. That is apart from Mr Brownlee. He likes formality. I think you would say he is stiff-upper-lipped."

"I know Mr Brownlee. He's a regular in the café. Used to read the newspaper every day. Now he has other distractions…he's not as stiff as you perhaps think…or maybe he is!"

"I don't understand."

"Well, before I board the ship on Saturday I'll pop in and tell you about it."

Needless to say, Sheila didn't win the lottery that night, but she did pop round to the newsagents the next evening after she closed up the café. The newsagents stayed open longer than the café but they were still drinking tea, chatting and laughing two hours after Sandeep closed the shop. They talked about the weird and wonderful customers they both experienced and some of their own amusing anecdotes dealing with the general public.

Over the next few weeks, they met up, mainly at the newsagents after Sheila had finished work. She would help out Sandy by organising the storeroom and making drinks, and eat the odd cake that she brought from the café. Once a week, when Sheila had a deep clean at the café, Sandy would close up the newsagents a little earlier and help her with the cleaning.

About six weeks into this working relationship, they were in the newsagent's small stock room piling unsold newspapers together for re-cycling when their bodies accidently brushed up against each other. Then, within a few minutes, their bodies touched again and then again. Before very long their lips and hands were touching.

That was over four months ago. Their meetings were now usually four or five times a week but the timings of their meetups were flexible, depending on their needs and wants.

***

"Are you OK Sheila?" asked Gwen standing at the counter. "You look as if you're miles away."

"Sorry, Gwen. I was…well not so much miles away, years away…"

"Oh?"

"Just having a bit of a mid-life moment, you know. What I've done with my life and what I want to do in the future…that sort of thing…"

"Is it business worries? Are you thinking of giving up the café, if you don't mind me asking?"

"No, nothing like that, I love the café. I'm coping well financially. I suppose it's other stuff."

"Do you mean pleasure, then?"

"Yes, I've been in a sort-of relationship for a few months but we're keeping it very quiet and I'm not sure it can continue like this for much longer. It's as if we're both frightened to make it public or take the next step as it might ruin the magic."

"I see. Have you spoken to him about it?"

"No, not really…perhaps he likes it how it is."

"Or perhaps he feels the same way as you? You need to talk. You deserve to know where you stand. Take a chance. Have your cake and eat it. Talking of cake, can we have two slices of your Lemon Drizzle and a pot of tea for two." Gwen looked over at Ray. "We took a chance and we are eating cake now." Both women smiled.

"I think…no, I know you're right. I have feelings for this man. I will send him a text, see him tonight and tell him how I feel."

"Why don't you go now. If my suspicions are correct about who it is, it won't take you very long to walk there, have a twenty minutes' chat and then be back here in less than thirty minutes. Ray and I can look after the café in the meantime."

Sheila smiled and put on her coat. "Thank you Gwen. I won't be long. Wish me luck." And with that, Sheila headed for the door.

***

During the time that Sheila was gone, Ray made the drinks and washed up while Gwen served the customers and delivered the orders to the tables. They made a great team and had fun doing it.

It was about fifty minutes before Sheila returned. Behind her was Sandeep.

"Well, look at you two. I ought to leave you in charge more often. Thank you Gwen and Mr Brownlee."

"Please, both of you, call me Ray. You're friends now."

"Well thank you, Ray and Gwen, and can I formally and informally introduce you to my boyfriend Sandeep… he prefers to be called Sandy. We've decided to go public on our relationship, thanks to you both," as Sheila spoke, Sandy held Sheila's hand and pecked her on the cheek.

"Hello both," said Sandy, "it's lovely to properly meet you both as a couple. You must think we've been stupid, being so secretive. But now, we are also a couple and we're not afraid of telling people. I must get back to the shop, but we bought you a small thank-you present," he continued and placed a jar of strawberry jam on the counter. "Perhaps, one day soon, we can have breakfast together as a foursome?"

"That would be lovely. Jam on toast all round?" suggested Gwen.

"Actually, I prefer Marmite, but I can be persuaded," said Sandy, smiling.

PASSING WOMEN

The Question

My question to you is this…
What is your greatest wish for your child?
To be happy, to be successful, to have a family maybe?
The list goes on
But one wish that's often neglected, or purposely omitted, is this:
I want my child to out-live me…by a long time.

Sadly, for some of us, that wish doesn't come true.
Death shouldn't take a younger life away from an older life,
But it does.

Tragically, death can play a sickening hand in a young person's life.
Sometimes the insides of a young body just cannot cope with the stuff
that life throws at them from the outside – germs, diseases, tumours…
Sometimes, it's just the internal workings of a young body that stops
working.
It gives up and a young heart stops.
It's outside of the control of a parent
And the parent has to give up their child.

Then there are the young people who die by the hands of others
Intentional, unintentional, youthful stupidity,
Hands on a trigger, hands off a steering wheel, hands on a drug.

Any death of a child is unnatural.
But the most unnatural act of all is when young people end their own
lives.
Leaving their parents alive but dead inside.
With the knowledge their children cannot face another day of living.
They would prefer an eternity of death.
Leaving behind unanswered questions and gaps
Why? What did I do? What did I not do? Why not me instead? If
only…

That's how it was with my daughter.
That's how it is with my daughter.
My beautiful, loving and caring girl,
Selfless to the end,

And yet uncharacteristically and unknowingly
She committed the ultimate selfish act.

I know I shouldn't use the word 'committed'
When talking about suicide.
It implies a sin or a crime,
But if feels like it to me.
Even if the act is no longer illegal
In the eyes of modern day thinking,
Where freedom of choice conquers all.
The act of suicide frees you from your own prison cell.
There is no jail time for the victim,
Quite the opposite,
It's the family who do the time.

I am told by well-intentioned strangers
That my daughter did not "commit suicide."
Instead "Your daughter died by or from suicide"
And "Your daughter ended or took her own life."
Apparently, somehow, this sounds better,
But not to me.

The cold, hard pages of a dictionary
will tell you that suicide is
"The intentional taking of one's life."
It sounds like my daughter was a thief.
In a way, I suppose, she did steal something from me.

Suicide is not a victimless crime, but a crimeless victim of the system,
Existing in lock down.
The door is opened
Free to run free
But stopped for good at the gate,
A late arrival and an early departure.

But as much as I want to tell you about how I feel,
This is about my daughter.
My daughter who left me,
Without a final goodbye or explanation,
Without any last or lasting words.

So my words are our words,
My story is our story.

But I can only give you my side of the story.
I would love to know what her story would say
And how different it would it be to mine.

So please make a note of this grieving mother.
I'm powerless to put things right,
Powerless to change the past now.
All I have are these words.

My daughter's name is Melissa, was Melissa,
No, she is still Melissa. She lives on.
She was, is, beautiful inside and out.

She passed away two months before her eighteenth birthday.
The birthday celebration that most teenagers long for,
The golden age of adulthood,
The age of uncaged freedom,
The magical time of can do, not can't do,
A time of so many possibilities.

That's not to say that Melissa didn't have possibilities.
When she was a child and in her early teens
She had choices and it seemed that she made the right ones.

She considered her family as friends,
And her friends as family.
She had a joyous sense of humour
Finding fun in other people
And happy to be the butt of her own jokes.

Melissa was a bright light that glistened
In the classroom, in the playground,
On stage, and in her bedroom with friends.

But somewhere along the way her light diminished,
All that glistened was no longer gold.
Her face was not as brave.
Her words dried up.
The special girl in my life regarded herself
As nothing special.
Doubts crept in. Never satisfied.
Love turned to hate.
Hate turned inwards.
Somewhere, somehow, she lost her way.

I looked on at a parental distance
Seeing it as a passing phase,
A pity stop on the road to maturity,
Sooner rather than later it would end,
And it did.

The day came when Melissa
Could no longer see the road ahead.

How her life stopped and where her life stopped
Are too painful to write down.

Since that day and over the years
I have read and listened to so many parents' accounts,
Describing their experiences
The last movements and moments of their children's lives.
What they did, when they did it.

I know these details about Melissa
But no-one else needs to know.
I only want to know why.
And I don't know the answer to that,
And I know I never will.

When I try to answer the 'why' question
It becomes a spiralling blame game.
It starts with me, then,
Her family,
Her friends,
Her teachers,
Her so-called friends,
The internet,
Her virtual friends,
And back to me,
Always back to me.

I don't blame Melissa.
I forgive her. Every day.
But I get angry with her at times
Now that she's apart from me.
She left me,
She left me alone
With a question unanswered,

A blank answer sheet with a cross at the end.

I feel like a failure, my lovely daughter.
I failed you, Melissa.

The Answer

Oh mom, dear mom,
I know you want answers,
I know you want to understand,
But this is the only answer I have...

It wasn't your fault.
Don't blame yourself.
It was my decision.
You raised me to think and act for myself,
And that is what I did.

I'd like to tell you that, on reflection, I was wrong,
I made a mistake.
I was confused, irrational, too impetuous.
Perhaps I was.
Perhaps I should let the living try to explain.

All I can say for now
Is that I don't hurt, I don't feel pain,
I don't feel isolated, anymore.
But it wasn't you that made me feel like that, mom.
Please believe me.
You were the only one that kept me going.

Am I happier now?
I can't remember what happy was.
But I don't feel sad either, just numb.
No more lows and occasional highs.
A flat line of feelings.

My only worry is about
The people who I left behind.
The people who will think that it was their fault
Particularly you, mom.

I feel so guilty.
I've ruined your life by improving mine.

That's just not fair. I'm selfish.
You're right, mom.
But there was no alternative.
Despite what others say.

Mom, I wasn't selfish on that day.
I didn't act impulsively on that day.
I had thought long and hard about my decision,
And I came to the conclusion
That the world didn't want me or need me,
And I didn't need the world.

I couldn't cope with that pain, anymore.
So, I killed the pain.
But unfortunately, I just passed the pain on.

If only I could assure you, mom,
That I made the correct decision.

This might not be the answer that you want or need.
But it's all I can give you, along with your memories of me.

I hope you can cope with the pain
That I've passed on to you.

I should have explained this to you while I was alive,
But as my mother you would have tried to convince me
That life was worth living.
That things would get better.
But living wasn't for me.

Death suits me better,
Because I couldn't get any better.

Life is a passing phase…
A choice, a chance, a lottery.
But I don't feel that I lost,
Neither did I win,
I somehow served my time.
It may have been short
But it was enough,
More than enough.

I wonder if I'd have had a daughter
Would I have outlived her?

By doing what I did
Have I spared her the pain?
Perhaps...who knows?
I'm sure my answer
Won't satisfy anyone.
Particularly you, mom.
As I did not pass your exam question,
I failed the test.
But mom, you never failed me.
Never.

II
DEAD BEATS

THE FAILING MAN

Climb the stairs as far as you can go,
So that you can look down at the view.
Solid square blocks and moving dots.
Then look across at all the possibilities
As far as the eye can dream.

The climb has been tough,
One small step at a time,
Keep moving onwards and upwards,
Don't stop now,
Keep believing, have no doubts,
That with every step, at every level,
There will be an escape.

The body tires, short breaths,
As you climb inside the dizzy heights,
Hoping to reach the top
Then you can stop
And breathe the rarified air.

Why didn't you turn around?
Was it your ego?
Was it your ambition
That pushes you on?

Maybe I've reached the top?
Perhaps I should look at the view.

I pause and reflect through the windows.
It looks no better from up here.
The future is no more clear or certain.
It feels further out of reach.

I look down at the ground.
I see myself as a small dot.
If only I could climb again
From a different starting point,
But it's too late!

Is this my view?
Is this my here and now?

If it is,
Then, I should count my blessings
From ground zero upwards.

But if I go back
I could count my steps
Head long and at speed.

Or maybe I'll be caught
As I fall from grace,
Frozen in time.
No name or regrets,
Even for the failing man.

All Men,
Named and nameless,
Fail in time
And fall from grace
And the human race.
Even The Falling Man
9/11

BRICKS AND MORTALS

On a bright February morning in middle England
A middle-class couple
Instruct a team of trusted builders
To demolish
Their relatively new kitchen
And replace
With new bricks, mortar and granite.
The end of their world
Is prevented by a bank transfer.
Home improved
By the cost of materials and labour.
A small skip
Rubble neatly stacked and taken away.
Buried underground.

On the same morning somewhere else

A mother wakes her children
From their slumbers and dreams,
There were
screams and tears
Shock, panic and fears

As the house came crashing down
An unnatural disaster

Sleep patterns changed
Never to be the same

Bricks scattered
Lives shattered
Years to re-build

Never to forget
A long labour

Millions of bricks and mortals
Across Turkey, Syria, Ukraine and elsewhere
Rubble burying the dead

Ruining the past and present
Scarring the future
Homes
decline.

In the end
Castles are made of sand.
They are built proud and tall
But inevitably fall
At the hands
Of Mother Nature, Father Time
And War Crimes.
Anywhere, any time
Nothing survives
The test of time.
Just ashes and dust,
Just perceptions and perspectives.

SLIPPING AWAY

You are haunted by the fear of missing out
At an early age.
"It's past your bedtime."
"Just ten more minutes…please."
"It's past your bedtime."
"Can I just have another chapter…please?"

You enjoy the next few chapters
"Haven't you got a home to go to?"
"I haven't finished my drink yet."
You sip your grown-up beer,
The last one to leave,
The last one to go to bed.

In time, the beer tastes better.
Through the blur you see her clearly,
She sips away at her glass,
You suggest they slip away,
You are the first ones to leave,
The first ones to get to bed.

You both stand around the side,
 Trying to smile at the younger ones
Drinking and dancing at your retirement party,
You glance at your watch and touch it,
It's the sign to slip away.
Without a fuss, without missing out.
They won't notice we've gone.

She holds my hand at the hospital,
Telling me bed side stories,
"You'll get better"
"There's time for another chapter"
She glances at her watch,
It's stopped.
It's the sign for me to slip away.

She invites everybody back to her house
After the funeral,
And the younger guests stand around the side

Holding a glass without even a sip
"He'll be sadly missed"
Glancing at watches,
Waiting for a sign
To slip away.

THE BEAT GOES ON

The Little Drummer Boy

He's one of a band of brothers
But sits behind the others
Often obscured, furthest away
But continues to make them play
Pa rum pum pum pum

The spotlight shines front of stage
But fades on him with time and age
Backs turned on him during the show
Their stature casts a lonely shadow
Pa rum pum pum pum

But they need him to be there
To be rhythm and pace aware
They hear his beating heart
Playing a minor but major part
Pa rum pum pum pum

He can see them for what they are
Plucky fiddlers and shooting stars
Loud mouthing any old anthem
While he watches and listens out for them
Pa rum pum pum pum

Beating down his stretched skin
Each night he counts them in
From the tunes of the past
To the new that won't last
Pa rum pum pum pum

And so the band plays on … pa rum
While the songs remain the same … pum pum pum
But the little drummer boy … pa rum
Upbeat or downbeat … pum pum pum
Plays his part … pa rum
To the final encore … pum pum pum
To the final note … pa rum
And then stands up … pum pum pum

Dwarfing the others on stage
His heart beating in its cage … pum pum pum
Taking a well-deserved rest
Puffing out his chest … pum pum pum
He and his drum
Pa rum pum pum pum
He and his drum
Pa rum pum pum pum

To Clive Brown
A larger-than-life drummer and man

Different Drum

James Beck Gordon (1945 – 2023)
Jim Gordon was an American musician and songwriter. He was a highly respected and sought-after drummer who played with acts including Derek and the Dominoes, Traffic, Frank Zappa, Steely Dan, George Harrison and Harry Nilsson.
In the 1970s Jim Gordon began to hear voices (including his mother's) compelling him to starve himself and stop playing the drums. His physicians misdiagnosed his problems and treated him for alcohol abuse.
In 1983, in a psychotic episode associated with his undiagnosed schizophrenia, Gordon attacked his mother with a hammer and a knife. He claimed that a voice had told him to kill her.
Gordon was sentenced to sixteen years in prison. He was denied parole ten times and died in prison in March 2023 at the age of 77.

From an early age
He would beat himself up
Trying to beat the clock
To keep pace with the others.

He would be on time
Or ahead of his time

Every session, every day
A shining star in the limelight
Every concert, every night
A dark star in the spotlights

He played with them all
Behind the scenes
Behind the screams

He supported them all

He would be on time
Or ahead of his time

He was a domino
He was a mother of invention
He navigated the traffic
Even though he was a mad dog

As the praise and plaudits
Drummed in his ears
The music led to beers,
Tears and fears

He missed many beats
Time after time

He became two people
In one body
He heard the music
And the voices

His invented mother
Stopped him sleeping
Stopped him relaxing
Stopped him drumming
The songs in his head
Told him to use his hands
To beat a different drum
And it finished with a
Hammer blow and a stab.

Half way into his life
Half way through his drum solo
He was sentenced, imprisoned
And diagnosed as a mad dog
Two mad dogs
The first half of his life sentence
The one mad dog played the beats
The second half of his life sentence
The other mad dog locked in his kennel
Never to be allowed out
Until his beating heart stopped

"If a man does not keep pace with his companions, perhaps it is because he hears a different drummer. Let him step to the music he hears, however measured or far away."
Henry Thoreau

CAKE

If the moon is made of cheese,
Then it's hard cheese.

But if the Earth is made of cake,
It would be sponge cake.
Made from the finest ingredients,
Baked with care,
At just the right temperature.
Then just left to cool.
Before the icing goes on the top
In white, blue and green.
We place the candles on the top
To celebrate the years
And warms the cake again.

We close our eyes
And Make a wish
To be older and wiser.
We open our eyes again
But the lights have faded
As we grow older but not wiser.

Once, the cake looked perfect,
Until it was sliced and diced
Into unequal portions.

Beneath the surface
Parts are undercooked
Some parts overbaked
Slowly melting.

In time the sponge is stale
Unappetising.
Inedible.
So the master bakers
Look up to the heavens
With greedy stares
At the spinning wheel of hard cheese.

While the rest of us

Eat the cake
And wait for our
Just desserts.

TRAFFIC LIGHTS

At a certain age
We pass the test of time
And slow down
So when we see red
There is no rage
Against the light
We apply the brakes
By mutual consent
And obey the code
We have less journey time
But we still wait patiently
Aware of other travellers
We don't cross the line
And then there's the others
In the rear-view mirror
On roads less travelled
Displaying shades of amber and green
Pointing in different directions
They gear up, foot pumping,
Hands braced in fists
Ready to fly
First off the blocks
Emergency stop
One add one
Makes two to tangle
Then head on or head off
Who started it?
Witness statements
Re-live the event
Apart from the dead
The rest turn their heads
Stare at the scene
And then drive on again
There is no stopping
As all is forgotten

TIME AND TIDES

Dona

My name is Dona. I from Philippines. I am 24 years.
I speak a little English. But not much.
I try to learn from people I meet.
I meet a lot of men I work for.
I am, how do you say, an escort?

Most men look after me
But some are cruel.
When I was sixteen
One man burned me,
Left some scars,
But I carried on.

I carry the load
Of too many men now.
They weigh me down.
Nobody looks after me.
I'm on my own.
I feel used and abused.
No-one cares.

I thought I met a nice man,
His name was Vector.
But one day he hit me
And I was left to die.
No-one came to my rescue.

I was buried
Beneath the surface
Of other news and blame.

No-one heard my story,
No-one read my story.
The rest of the world
Was deaf and blind
To this part of the world,
Because it doesn't count.

They couldn't and wouldn't

Count the lives lost,
Only the few that survived.
The rest are nameless,
Including me.

My name is MV Dona Paz.
I am a passenger ferry.
On 20th December 1987
I was carrying well over 3,000 people,
2000 more than I should have been carrying.
I collided with an oil tanker, MT Vector.
At 22.30 in the Tablas Strait, Phillipines
I sank within two hours.
Only 24 souls survived.

"The Deadliest Peacetime Maritime Disaster"
And yet very few people know about the MV Dona Paz
But, somehow, we all know about The Titanic.

I lie here on the sea bed
And I wonder why.

Breaking The Safety Glass
My ancestors were not explorers.
They moved in small circles.
They didn't invade others' spaces,
Consequently, no-one bothered them.
Every time of night and day was the same.
It was all they knew.
No memories of the past,
Nothing to remind them.
No thoughts of the future
Of how it could or should be.

That was until the visitors arrived.
Just one alien ship from up above
Landing on the surface.
My parents and grandparents
Stared at it from a distance
Too scared to go near.
It seemed out of place and out of time.

Eventually, they accepted it
And it became part of the scenery.
Old, tired, rusting and seemingly forgotten
Dead to the whole world.

It was left to me, many years later,
To see the outsiders returning.
Wanting to investigate
Explore further and make contact.
But these visitors failed again,
Leaving just another remainder on the seabed.
A reminder for my offspring
To steer clear from the unknown.

You may think that we are
A shoal of fools,
But we know our limits.

Perhaps we should all live
Inside our own goldfish bowls
And not break the safety glass.

For those lost souls on board The Titanic (1912) and the Titan submersible
(2023).
They pushed the boundaries beyond human limits
and died among the fish.

Glyn
Glyn avoided the war
And the war avoided him.
Unstable and unreliable,
Not able to stand on his own two feet,
And yet he became a war hero,
Buried with full military honours.

Abandoned by this father.
Left by his mother.
Glyn drifted to London
From the Rhondda Valley.
Lonely, destitute, homeless,
A nobody on the streets.
When the German bombs fell

He hadn't the strength to shelter.
Others would pass him by
And assume he was collateral,
Dead to the war and the world.

Glyn dreamt of a different life
In a different time,
A place where he was a somebody,
Successful, admired.
But in his darkest moments,
Often while eating scraps of bread
With hatred falling from above
And apathy all around him,
He considered death
As his only way to escape.
Perhaps the world would be
A better place without him.

But Glyn became some body.
Prepared for the role of his life,
He drifted to the coastline of Spain,
And under the cover of deception
He played a starring part
In stopping
Another war to end all wars.

Glyn never was
The man who never was.
He was some body.

Glyn was not just any body
Who was more use dead than alive.
He was stable, reliable.
He could stand on his own two feet,
And he could swim not sink.

But it is only now, many years later
Through books, films and plays
That we pay tribute to a fallen man.

And as the waves
Return to the ocean,
Glyn still waves at us,

At peace with himself.

Glyndwr Michael, (often referred to as "The Man Who Never Was"), was a troubled man who ended up living on the streets in London in the early 1940s. When he died in January 1943, Glyn's body was used by the British Military Intelligence to create a plan that lured German forces to Greece, prior to the Allied invasion of Sicily. Glyndwr Michael's corpse became Major William Martin, a British Officer carrying misleading top secret military documents, was washed up on the shores of neutral Spain. German Military Intelligence was completely deceived by Operation Mincemeat, as it was known, and the plan was a strategic success and significantly contributed to the Allies winning the Second World War.

After the true identity of Glyn's body was confirmed in 1996, Glyndwr Michael and 'William Martin' now share a single grave in Huelva, Spain.

Acknowledgements

The pieces in this anthology aim to examine the fragility of life and relationships and what remains afterwards.

I would like to acknowledge everyone who, in some way or another, has contributed to these stories or poems. In most cases you don't know who you are, or unfortunately, you are no longer with us.

A special thank you to Di Lees and Ann for their valuable insights when critiquing my writing.

The Author

Ian Meacheam has spent most of his working life in education. He was a teacher of English and Drama in secondary schools in Solihull. He then became a school advisor in Birmingham working in the School Improvement department.

Ian has written two novels and several anthologies of short stories and poetry.

Ian lives in Lichfield with his wife Ann. They have one son, David, who is married to Tayla. Ian and Ann also have two wonderful grandchildren – Matilda and Alexander.

Printed in Great Britain
by Amazon